"Jolene, you know that kiss meant something. And I know those feelings were mutual, too."

"But that doesn't mean we can get carried away."

Trent stepped back, hands up in surrender.

"Please stay. I promise I won't try to kiss you."

"Again."

"*Again*," he added begrudgingly. "If you go, I'm going to have to follow to make sure you get home safely. And I'd much rather stay here in front of the fire."

Jolene stared at Trent for a long moment, still slightly flushed.

"I'm not going to sleep with you tonight."

"Fine, I don't want you to anyway," Trent replied, too quickly.

Jolene smirked. "Okay then, I'll stay."

"Good." Trent turned and left the room before his mouth—and hers—got him into any more trouble. Besides, he needed a minute to cool off, and to wrap his mind around the fact that they were two big, fat liars.

Dear Reader,

One Christmas, after presents were opened and breakfast was eaten, my father took a chain saw to our Christmas tree, then burned it.

Oh, there's a story there, of course. I grew up in Houston, where some Decembers don't get below sixty degrees. Our lovely Christmas tree had been "lovely" until about December 18th. By then, the warm weather had gotten to it. In short, our tree had become a fire hazard.

What's unusual about this event was that no one in my family was terribly shocked about seeing a chainsaw in our living room on December 25. All we did was put the ornaments in their boxes and get out of the way! My family wasn't known for Norman Rockwell moments by any stretch of the imagination.

Perhaps this is why I was so excited to write a Christmas romance with a fairly untraditional couple. I really liked Jolene Arnold, with her sassy nature and her show-stopping legs. I liked Trent, who was gorgeous and just a little bit of a jerk. But most of all, I loved how they made their Christmas wonderful, even if it wasn't all that perfect. I hope you enjoyed their romance, too.

I also hope you have a wonderful holiday season. I wish you happiness, good health, a bit of laughter… and, most of all, someone special to share those moments with.

Merry Christmas!

Shelley Galloway

My Christmas Cowboy

SHELLEY GALLOWAY

TORONTO NEW YORK LONDON
AMSTERDAM PARIS SYDNEY HAMBURG
STOCKHOLM ATHENS TOKYO MILAN MADRID
PRAGUE WARSAW BUDAPEST AUCKLAND

Recycling programs
for this product may
not exist in your area.

ISBN-13: 978-0-373-75383-3

MY CHRISTMAS COWBOY

Copyright © 2011 by Shelley Sabga

Chapter One

Jolene ran a finger along the note her friend Cheryl
had stuck on the front of her apartment door. Trent
Riddell was back in town, and Cheryl had even found
his unlisted phone number.

Now, didn't that beat all?

She didn't know whether to spit nails or thank the
Lord Almighty.

She settled on talking to her baby girl.

"Amanda Rose, what do you think about that? After
all this time, I guess we're finally going to get to recon-
nect with Mr. Wonderful himself."

As she heard her words, thick with sarcasm, even she
felt a little embarrassed. Being bitchy wasn't like her.

Of course, being ignored wasn't something she'd
ever done real well, either.

"When do you think we should pay him a call, sugar?
Tomorrow morning? Next week?"

The baby didn't answer her, of course, which was
really just as well. There was no right time to introduce
a man to his unexpected offspring.

But, come to think of it, there should be. Dear Abby
or Emily Post or somebody ought to write some directions about stuff like that. If they did, she'd snap them

up right away. She wasn't a fool, she needed all the help she could get.

Feeling the urge for a cigarette, she quickly snatched a piece of bubble gum from her cavernous purse. She pulled off the wrapper and chomped down hard. As sweetness infused her mouth, Jolene tried to pretend the jolt of sugar was almost as satisfying as that first rush of nicotine.

Yes, giving up smoking had been the right thing to do. Smoking was bad for her health. Expensive, too.

But somehow all she could think about was the sugar that was no doubt rotting her teeth that very minute. And she sure as heck couldn't afford to go to the dentist.

What she needed was a plan.

Well, there was no time like the present. She just had to dive right in. Make plans. Carefully, she dug in her purse again, this time coming up with her cell phone. After taking a deep breath, she dialed before she lost her nerve. She had to at least try.

Maybe she'd get lucky and only reach his voice mail. She really had no business talking to Trent. Especially since the last time they'd seen each other, well, they really hadn't done all that much talking. Their lips had been busier doing other things.

Besides, she had a very good idea that Trent wasn't going to be all that happy with her news.

"Yeah?"

His voice was brusque. Distracted. Downright rude. Well, at least he'd answered! "Trent?"

"Yeah. Who's this?"

Mildly irritated, she matched his tone and decided to stick in his middle name to show him she wasn't fooling around. "Trent Wallace Riddell, this is Jolene Arnold."

"Jo?" He coughed. "Hey. Um, how you doing?" His voice went from brusque to hesitant.

She knew why. He was afraid she was calling because she wanted to hook up with him again.

She did not. She just wanted to let him know that they were now bonded for life, thanks to a pint-size blond baby.

Or maybe Trent was afraid she had feelings for him.

She did not. Well, not the romantic kind.

Or maybe he was afraid that she wanted something from him.

She did. But it wasn't what he thought. She didn't want his loving or his kisses or his money. He deserved to know he was a daddy. And her daughter deserved to be claimed as a Riddell.

"I'm better than you, I think," she said with more bluster than an August wind. "I just heard through the grapevine that you're laid up something awful."

"Yeah. A bull got the best of me," he mumbled.

"What's hurt?"

He grunted under his breath. "What isn't?" A little louder, he said, "I'm not too banged up."

"Define 'too.'"

"Arm's broken. A few ribs got busted up, but they're mending."

"Your poor body. You had a mess of bruises last time we saw each other."

"Did I? I don't remember."

Well, that was a bit insulting. Her cheeks flushed with the memories. They'd visited a while at Bronco Bob's when she was through with her shift, talking more with each shot of Jack. One thing led to another, that led to them getting naked on her apartment floor.

She cleared her throat and firmly instructed herself to move things forward. "I'm real sorry you got hurt."

"Ain't no big deal. Every once in a while, the bull gets the upper hand. It's all part of the job."

"Some job."

"You know I love it. But still…I appreciate your concern."

Jolene heard the question at the end of his statement, and she knew what it meant, too. He didn't understand why she'd tracked him down.

They weren't all that close anymore. And they hadn't been close for years. Except for the drunk sex and such…

Taking care to keep her voice slow and nonchalant, she ventured, "So, I was thinking maybe I could come by and say hey. You know, see how you're doing in person."

There was a pause, then she heard some shuffling. "There's no need for that…"

"Actually, I think there is. I've got something we need to talk about."

"You do?" Obviously he was at a loss for words.

Just the thought of him at a loss for anything made Jolene smile. From the first day they'd met outside their houses on the way to kindergarten, that man had had confidence to spare.

Well, he wasn't the only one. She had confidence to spare, too. That was how she'd managed to have a good life for herself. It certainly wasn't because she'd been waiting around for cowboys to step up and take care of her.

As sweet Amanda Rose gurgled a bit in her carrier, Jolene got to business. "How about I stop on by your

house later on tonight?" After all, there was no time
like the present.

Yeah. Just like Trent, she was gonna take that old
bull by the horns.

"Tonight?"

"That wouldn't be a problem, would it? I won't stay
long."

"Oh. Well, then. Seven o'clock would work."

"Great. I'll be seeing you in a few hours with bells
on." As she looked at her tiny Christmas tree, chock-full
of red and green lights, she smiled. "With Christmas
bells."

"Hey, wait a minute, Jo…"

She didn't miss the new hint of foreboding in his
voice. "Yes?"

"I don't want to sound like an ass or anything, but I'm
not really lookin' to start up a relationship or nothing."

She chewed on that ball of gum in a real effort to
keep her voice even. "Don't worry, Trent. I'm not looking to start up anything, either." After all, what they'd
started was sitting right by her side, looking as cute as
a june bug in August.

After they finished their goodbyes, Jolene closed the
phone and stood up. It was four o'clock. She had three
hours to put herself together and look like the person she
wanted to be in his life—his friend. And, she needed
to look like the person she already was: the mother of
his child.

TRENT HUNG UP THE PHONE and stared at it, bemused.
Jolene Arnold. Well, now. He hadn't expected to hear
from her.

She was a pretty thing, and always had been. Scrappy

and thin. Curly blond hair, bright greenish-brown eyes, soft skin, and the kind of figure that made a man think about pinup girls. Oh, but she had a fine pair of legs. A great ass, too.

He'd seen many a man watch her backside in admiration whenever she took a walk downtown. Or when she waited tables at Bronco Bob's.

He would know, because one night he'd been one of them.

Of course, rumor had it that she'd made many a man happy, period. Even him, much to his shame.

For that, he was ashamed. His whole family had always had a soft spot for her, ever since she'd confessed at age six that no one had ever read her a story.

After that, both his parents had looked out for her when it became evident that no one with the last name of Arnold was going to do that job.

Now his mother would be jumping out of her grave and boxing his ears well and good if she had any idea how he'd treated Jolene. He shouldn't have given in to too much booze and acted on that very bad idea that had actually been very, very good.

But no matter what they shared—or how many things they shouldn't have done—Trent knew Jolene was always going to claim a soft spot in his heart. He'd met her on the way to the school bus their first day of kindergarten. Trent had been tagging behind Cal Jr. and Jarred, and she'd been tagging behind him.

She'd had on a red dress and black Mary Janes and a bow in her hair. He'd thought she was as cute as a button.

As the months went by, she'd taken to coming over to their house most every afternoon. Soon, she was almost like a Riddell shadow. Even Jarred didn't seem to mind if she sat beside him while he did his homework.

If they wanted to talk, she'd talk. If everyone was busy, she'd sit and color. She never mentioned her home, and one day when he was talking about it, asking how come they never went to her house to play, Junior had pulled him to one side and told him to shut up.

"Things aren't good over there, Trent. That's why she's here."

And his brother Jarred had gone one better. "Just be nice to her. And make sure she eats, too."

When he was small, he'd never really understood what was wrong. By the time they were in fourth grade, he'd had a real good idea of what went on in that house. And then, just when he was thinking that he needed to do something about her situation, his dad struck oil.

They'd moved into their current big house. Months later, Jolene had moved away when her daddy couldn't pay his bills.

He hadn't seen her in ages until he'd spied her working at Bronco Bob's. He'd hugged her tight and kissed her cheek when he figured out who she was.

After that, it was only natural to share a beer. And a couple of shots of Jack Daniel's. Next thing he knew, their talking led to his truck, which led to her apartment, which led to them getting stark naked and rolling around on the floor for a while.

Hours later, when the taste of Jack had turned sour in his mouth and the reality of what they'd done had hit him hard, he'd been embarrassed.

She'd been quiet.

He'd pulled on his jeans and had left in a hurry. Promised to call.

But he'd been lying, of course. No matter what city or two-bit town he was in, he didn't call after rolls in the sack. It wasn't his way.

So when she started calling him, he figured it would be best to ignore those calls. After all, he wasn't in love. And, well, he was "Trent Riddell" now. That name meant something. He was rich and he was famous.

He did not need some blonde from his past bringing him down.

But that didn't stop the moments on the tour bus or in his hotel room when he'd remember how sweet kissing Jolene had been. How her eyes had turned all sparkly when they'd reminisced about tromping through the fields back when they were small.

Luckily, it had only taken a couple of hours to not care anymore. Because even though Jolene Arnold had once been his friend and had even for a few hours been his lover…she sure as hell didn't mean all that much to him now.

Really, she was just a memory.

Chapter Two

"Trent? Trent, you home?" Ginny called out as she let the back door slam behind her.

Trent was just about to answer when another voice rang through the house. "Virginia Anne, I swear, you're going to be the death of me," their father bellowed seconds later. "Trent Wallace?"

Trent scrambled to his feet and started toward the kitchen. Honestly, what was it with everyone calling him by his full name today? "Sir?" he asked.

"Look at your sister."

Dutifully, Trent looked. And then looked again. "Ginny, you're covered in mud."

His father cussed, "No shit, Sherlock."

To Trent's astonishment, Ginny didn't even flinch. If anything, she looked about ready to roll out her own list of profanities.

"What happened?" Walking forward, he stuck out his right hand—the one not contained in a brace—and lifted her chin. "Is that a black eye?"

"Uh-huh. But Peter's got one, too."

Trent couldn't care less what some little pip-squeak was sporting. "A boy's been beating up on you? Dad, who's Peter?"

But instead of looking worried, Cal Sr. just looked peeved. "Peter is the poor boy who's become Ginny's object of affection. She's been torturing him something awful." With a grimace, he pulled a pink note out of his back pocket. "Look at this."

Trent took the paper and scanned it. As he read it again, some of the terrible rage slipped away, only to be replaced by shock and awe. "Ginny's about to be suspended?"

"Worse than that. She's about to be kicked out of school for good."

Turning to her, he raised his eyebrows. "Virginia Anne, what the heck?"

But instead of looking cowed, she stuck up her chin. "It ain't my fault, Trent." When he continued to glare, she finally had the sense to lower her chin and the attitude. "Not all my fault, anyways."

"Not all your fault?"

"Peter deserved it. Some."

His sister had turned into some sort of itty-bitty bully. "Dad, what have y'all been doing with her? She needs some discipline."

"Oh, what in the Sam Hill haven't we been doing?" his dad retorted. "This is an ongoing thing, son. Your brothers and I have been doing the best we can with her. It's just a challenge, that's all."

"Can I go to my room now?" Ginny asked. "I want to go take a bath."

"Sure, honey. I'll be in to talk to you soon," their dad said wearily. When the room was empty, his dad leaned up against the wall and shook his head. "I never thought I'd say this, but I would have preferred five more boys than this one six-year-old girl. She's going to be the death of me."

When they were alone, Trent suddenly felt a whole lot less than six feet tall. "Guess I've been a little out of touch, huh? I had no idea y'all were struggling with her so much."

"Don't feel bad. You can't help that you weren't here. You've been on the circuit."

"Since I'm here now I'll start trying to do more."

"That's real good of you, son." He paused. "I better go make sure she actually got in the bathtub. And think of something to say to that girl."

Two things occurred to Trent. One, his father didn't expect him to follow through. And, even if he did follow through, his dad didn't think he'd be any good. "I'll go talk to her."

His dad paused on his way out the door. "Sure you're ready for that?"

"'Course. You go relax, now." He turned and walked upstairs to her room before he changed his mind. After ascertaining that she was in the bath, he told her to holler when she got out.

Fifteen minutes later, he was inside a room covered with enough pink, purple and horses that he felt as though he was living in the middle of some Barbie Dream House.

From the top of her comforter, his sweet-smelling sister watched him approach. "You mad at me, Trent?"

That made him pause. Was he? "I don't rightly know."

Obviously puzzled, she scrambled to a sitting position. "How come?"

"Well, your black eye for one. I hate to see my best girl hurt like you are."

"I'm not your best girl."

"And why's that?"

"You're never home."

Ouch. "My work takes me around the country, sister. I can't help that. And you watch that tone of voice with me, too. I may be a rookie at dealing with little girl fights, but I'm no pushover."

"I guess you're not."

Crossing the room, he sat next to her. "Here's what I don't get. How come you fight so much?"

Her eyes widened. "No one's ever asked me that before. They just told me to stop."

"You got an answer?"

"Maybe." When he crossed his arms over his chest, she eyed him carefully, then spoke. "Some days I'm just mad at everyone."

"And why's that?"

She lowered her voice. "Promise you won't get mad?"

He was probably a fool to promise such a thing, but he nodded.

"I get mad 'cause I don't have a mommy." Her voice turning stronger, she added, "And she didn't die and go to heaven like yours did. She took off 'cause she didn't want me."

If a bull had gone and kicked him in the head, Trent couldn't have been more winded. Valiantly, he tried to imagine what Jarred would say to that. Or Junior. Junior always had the right words.

But it was just him sitting there.

"I know," he finally said, and that was the truth. Carolyn, Cal Sr.'s second wife, might have hated their father, but she left her daughter without even a second look back.

Warily, he glanced at Ginny, half sure he'd just broken her heart. But instead of looking surprised, her eyes were a little wider—and trust was lingering there.

That suddenly made him a whole lot braver.

"Ginny, here's the deal. It's real sad that your momma took off. I don't know why she did, and maybe we'll never know. But growing up and being a good person means that you make do with what you have. And you have a whole lot more than most."

She blinked. "'Cause we live in a fancy house?"

"Nope. Fancy houses don't count for much at the end of the day. What counts are having people who love you. You've got a lot of those."

"Daddy and Jarred and Junior?"

"And me. And Serena and Susan and Gwen." He leaned back a little so he could look into her eyes. "You hear what I'm saying?"

"I guess so."

"Good. Now listen to this. You need to stop making everyone try so hard to do right by you. Next time you want to hit someone, you flat out got to make yourself stop. You hear me? What you're doing is mean and bad and you're making us all ashamed."

"But—"

"Ginny Riddell, Riddells don't hit. They don't go out of their way to be mean to folks. They try and listen. You're one of us, and I, for one, think it's about time you acted like it."

"And if I don't?"

Shoot. "And if you don't, I'm going to tell Santa

Claus to not even think about bringing anything for Ginny Riddell when he stops by this year."

Her mouth turned into a sweet little O. "You'd do that?"

"I certainly would. And I'd do it in a heartbeat, too."

Finally tears welled in her eyes. "I'll try to be better, Trent."

Though he wanted to cuddle her close, he knew all about wheedling ways. "Not good enough. You tell me that you're going to do better. That you *will* do better. Will you?"

"Yes."

"You'll be nicer and stop making everyone ashamed of you?"

"Yes."

"Good." Opening his arms, he beckoned her closer. "Now come over here and give me a hug, 'cause I love you."

"I love you, too, Trent."

With his arms wrapped around this little girl, for the first time in a long while, he felt proud of himself.

Chapter Three

In a perfect world, Jolene would've put on a nice pair of slacks and a neat, prim twin set for her big meeting with Trent. Sweet little hoops would have graced her ears. Her hair would have been flat-ironed and pretty, and she would have worn sensible shoes.

Most people would have been shocked to know that Jolene Arnold even knew about such things. But the truth was, she would've had no problem dressing up like something out of the latest J. C. Penney catalog. Well, she wouldn't if she'd had the extra money or temperament for such things.

Because the truth of the matter was that more often than not, she dreamed of being *that* girl.

That girl, *that nice girl.* The gal men took home to their mothers, not their beds. The one men dressed up for, took chew out of their cheeks for. The kind of woman where they watched their cussing and remembered their manners. The kind of person people showed up on time for.

But, as she looked in the mirror, Jolene figured that train had up and went sometime during the past decade. Truth was, her dreams of being the next June Cleaver had evaporated years before she'd even known who old June was.

Now all she had was a closet of sexy bar clothes and a Visa bill with baby items on it. So, she did the best she could with what she had. Looking in the mirror, she had to admit things could be worse.

On top, she had on a red Christmas sweater—the only one she had that wasn't cut low or was too tight. And on her bottom half, she was wearing one of her two pairs of slacks. The gray fabric didn't do a thing for her coloring, but the slacks were wool, not too worn, and almost loose. Boots were on her feet, because those were the best—and warmest—shoes she had.

And, of course, she had a baby on her hip.

As she looked at her reflection, she shrugged. Well, she wasn't exactly the cover girl for *Working Mother Magazine*.

But she could look worse. Maybe even Trent would start thinking she looked respectable.

Yeah, right.

Trent Riddell was going to take one look at her and ask what in the devil was she doing, standing on his doorstep.

"Not much I can do about it, though, Amanda," she said before turning away and picking up her purse and diaper bag. "I am what I am—and that's a very busy woman with a secret to reveal. Let's go get it over with."

After securing Amanda Rose in her car seat, Jolene spared a prayer that her car would start, and then slowly made the way through town and up toward the Riddell Ranch. She'd never been there, but she knew where it was. Shoot, everyone in North Texas did. Old Mr. Riddell had spent most of the past twelve years building a shrine to his family.

She'd even heard about it when she was waitressing in Dallas right after high school. Rumor had it that there was all kinds of gadgets there, and even an elevator. All in all, it was a real far step from the modest home they used to live in. Back when the Riddells lived next door to the Arnolds. Their homes had been carbon copies of each other. Plain old two bedroom homes with one bath and one living room.

Since then, things had changed a lot for both families. Too bad they'd veered in opposite directions, though. The difference was that old neighborhood had been the Riddells' worst place to live—while it had been Jolene's best until she'd gone out on her own and learned how to use her assets in the best way.

Thoughts of the past zipped away as she turned right onto Riddell Way, the made-up street name Mr. Riddell had put up at the beginning of their mile-long driveway. The closed gate at the front was a surprise, as was the little box that she had to push a button to talk into.

When she rolled her window down, a frozen patch of air whipped in and caught her by surprise. From the backseat, Amanda Rose let out a howl of displeasure. "I hear you, honey. Hold on now," she murmured before pressing on the button.

Two seconds passed before Trent's voice answered. "Yeah?"

"Trent, it's me. Jolene."

"Jolene?"

It was cold enough to set her nose to running, and her eyes watering, too. "Remember I told you I was coming by? I'm here."

"Oh. Hey, any chance you could come back later? I've kind of got my hands full."

And she didn't? "No, I cannot." Behind her, Amanda's little whines of protest morphed into a giant howl. She had to speak a little bit louder now because Amanda Rose was threatening to burst a lung. "Hush, baby."

"Baby? Who's that?"

"Baby is my daughter. She's cold because I've got the window down, talking to you," she added impatiently over Amanda Rose's carrying-on. "I'll explain everything as much as you need me to…later. Now open the darn gate."

Right away the gate opened.

"Praise the Lord for that," she muttered. She rolled up the window and inched forward before Trent changed his mind and closed the gates on her.

Amanda Rose continued to cry.

Oh, but a road had never seemed so long. As the baby wailed for all she was worth, Jolene's hands started to sweat as the house came into view.

All white and stately and gorgeous, it looked exactly like what any poor white trash Texan would produce, if he had a million dollars. A replica of J. R. Ewing's home from *Dallas*.

She parked in the circular driveway, grabbed her bag, and before she could chicken out, opened the back passenger door and unbuckled the baby. With Amanda in her arms and the carrier slung over an elbow, she marched up the steps and rang the doorbell.

Not two seconds passed before Trent opened the wide oak door decorated with the fanciest Christmas wreath she'd ever seen.

"Hey," he said.

It was cold. It was windy. Amanda Rose was crying for all she was worth.

But still Jolene was stunned into submission. Trent Riddell was a magnificent piece of man, and that was putting it mildly.

Dressed in dark jeans, black boots and a form-fitting indigo blue sweater, he looked like a model in an ad for men's cologne. He'd either forgotten to shave, or was fostering that Brad Pitt look. The one where men constantly looked scruffy.

Boy howdy, could he pull it off.

Her mouth went dry. Oh, what was it about Trent that made her wish she was something more?

"Hey," she said after way too long.

Looking irritated, he waved a hand across the threshold. "Well, come on in, Jo. You're gonna freeze your ass off if you stand out here much longer."

"Watch your mouth, Trent," she said testily as she walked on in. "I've got a baby here."

With a thud, the door closed behind her. "So I see."

Luckily, Amanda Rose had finally taken a breather and was happily nestled against her chest, looking at Trent as if he was her new favorite toy.

Unluckily, Trent leaned closer and grinned. The tangy scent of that cologne he should be modeling wafted closer. Mixing in with the scent of furniture polish and money that seemed to waft from every corner of the entryway.

"Well, let me see her." To Jolene's amazement, he held out his hands.

"Her name is Amanda Rose." She had no choice but to carefully place her baby—*their baby*—in his arms.

Jolene could hardly breathe as two sets of blue eyes

looked at each other in surprise. Two sets of dark blue eyes framed with inky black lashes.

The pissed off look he'd been sporting vanished in an instant. "She's a cutie, Jo. A real doll."

"Thank you."

As three-month-old Amanda stared up at him, raising one tiny fist up to his cheek, rubbing five o'clock shadow, Trent slowly turned her way. "So, who's the daddy?" His voice was husky. Uncertain. And...flat. "Do I know him?"

She noticed he didn't ask after her husband. Didn't even say boyfriend. No doubt he didn't expect that much of her.

It was time. "You."

He stepped backward fast. And his arms looked a little shaky, too. "What did you say?"

"Give her to me before you go and drop her."

He didn't hesitate, holding Amanda out in front of him like she was about to pee over the front of his shirt. "Jo..."

"Hold on a sec." Liking the unfamiliar feeling of being in control, she took her time setting down the carrier, settling Amanda in it, then crossing her arms in front of her chest and staring at Trent.

"Jolene, tell me I heard you wrong."

"You heard me right. I doubt any bull would be big enough to injure your hearing." Lowering her voice, she said, "This little ray of sunshine here is yours, cowboy. Or, maybe I should call you Daddy?"

Chapter Four

"Daddy?" A few choice colorful swear words erupted then.

As the air turned blue, Jolene waved a hand, as if clearing the air. "Oh, for heaven's sakes. Settle down, Trent. And watch your mouth."

"Dammit, Jo—what the hell are you doing, springing this on me like this?"

"I'm not springing a thing. I tried to let you know from the very beginning, but you would never return my calls."

"I would've returned them if I would've known this was what you were calling about."

"Why else would I have been calling you?"

His cheeks heated. "You know why."

"You are such a piece of work, Trent. Just to let you know, not every woman in the world thinks you're irresistible."

"You did."

Her voice rose. "I was drunk."

"So was I," he countered, giving it right back to her.

"Hold on, now! What's going on in here?" Mr. Riddell growled as he slowly entered the entryway, looking as if each step was paining him something awful.

"Nothing, Dad," Trent muttered.

His dad ignored him. Instead, he looked straight at her. Then smiled. "Jolene Arnold, is that you?"

"Yes, sir. It's nice to see you again, Mr. Riddell."

Trent looked as if he was about to pop a gasket. "Dad, really. This ain't a good time—"

That was really the wrong thing to say. Mr. Riddell glared at Trent. "Hush, son. Now, Jolene, you better get on over here and give me a hug."

Jolene picked up the carrier, stepped around the sputtering cowboy, and greeted Cal Riddell Sr. as though they were old friends.

Because that was what they were.

When they parted, Mr. Riddell said, "What brings you over here?"

"I came to see Trent."

"Oh?" He looked at Trent curiously. "You didn't tell me she was coming by."

Trent glared at her. "I didn't think she was going to be staying long."

"I won't stay long. All I needed to do was talk to you about Amanda Rose."

Mr. Riddell grinned at the baby. "So you're a mother now?"

She couldn't help but smile. "I am."

After a pause, Mr. Riddell slipped an arm around Jolene's shoulders and guided her into a swanky living room. When they stopped in front of a suede couch, he peered down at the baby. "She's a beauty, Jo. Amanda Rose, you said?"

"Yes, sir." Looking over her shoulder at Trent, who was standing in the doorway as though he was loitering, she raised an eyebrow.

He stared at her and scowled.

So she did the honors. "Mr. Riddell, her name is Amanda Rose Riddell."

Mr. Riddell's expression didn't waver a bit. Looking fondly at the baby, he leaned a little closer and ran one finger over Amanda's soft cheek. "Look at those eyes. Why, they are bluer than blue." He stopped abruptly and shot a good long look her way. "I'm sorry…what did you say?"

"Amanda is a Riddell. She's your granddaughter," she said softly. Feeling embarrassed and proud and suddenly shy.

Mr. Riddell stilled. "Trent?"

"We don't know that for sure. She just sprang the news on me," he said as he stepped forward. "Dammit, Jo. You're really going to do this…really?"

"Like I said, I've been trying to let you know. I must have called you two dozen times. But you wouldn't pick up the phone. She's your baby. She's our baby."

Trent looked pale as a ghost. "She might be mine. We won't know for certain until she gets tested."

"What?"

"I mean, I get tested," he sputtered. "Shit. I mean, hell, Jo. We gotta get a paternity test."

"Really? You think I'm making this up?"

"I mean there's no telling who the daddy is. Could be anyone…"

"Trent Wallace, you better watch your mouth…"

Slamming a palm on top of a very expensive coffee table, Mr. Riddell's voice turned low. "Enough of this nonsense. Look at her eyes, Trent. She's yours. Even if you don't believe me, those eyes ought to tell you the truth."

"She really is yours, Trent," Jo tried to explain. "I promise, I wouldn't say it if it wasn't true."

"And I'm telling you, I need proof."

When Trent stepped closer, his father looked him over as though he was no better than slime under a boot. "I've rarely been so disappointed in a son, Trent. You make this right."

Jolene's mouth went dry as Trent slumped right there in front of them both.

As she was trying to get her mind wrapped around that, Mr. Riddell engulfed her in a wiry hug. "She's a beautiful baby, Jolene. You should be proud."

"Thank you, sir."

"How 'bout you start calling me Cal? We're relatives, now," he said with a wink.

"Yes, sir. I mean, Cal."

He gave her another pat. "Now, don't you worry about a thing. Everything's going to be just fine, now. You're no longer alone."

Just like that, her eyes filled with tears. Trent's dad had known exactly the right words to say.

After pressing a kiss to her brow, he stepped away and glared at Trent one more time. "You and me will talk later."

When they were alone, Trent practically collapsed on the couch. "Great job, Jolene. Couldn't you have waited to involve my dad until I had at least two minutes to process the news?"

"This isn't my fault. You were there, too."

"Oh, I know." He ran a hand over his cheeks. "From what I recall, anyway." As the minutes ticked by, he rested his elbows on his knees and hung his head. "What do you want? Money?"

No way did she want to go lower in his estimation and be the trashy girl who was seeking him out only for money. She might not be the next June Cleaver, but she sure as hell wasn't *that* girl, either.

"I'm not sure."

"Come on, darlin'. You had to have had something in mind when you called me up and drove over here. I mean, good job. You got what you wanted, huh?"

Chin up, she stared right back at him. Oh, she hated that vaguely condescending, holier-than-thou tone of voice. No, she hadn't been a virgin when they'd gone at it all night long. But dammit, he hadn't been, either. Sometimes the double standards were enough to drive her nuts.

His eyes narrowed as the baby made a cute little cooing noise.

And because the only thing Jolene had ever had going for her was too much sass, she smiled. "I didn't plan on having a baby. But I did. And I don't regret it. Amanda Rose is the best thing I've ever done in my life and I'm proud of her. I'm her momma and I'm always going to be here for her. Always."

The look he gave her felt like a slap in the face. It was filled with sadness. With a touch of regret. With a sense that for a split second, he'd expected more from the girl who used to follow him around in kindergarten, and she'd disappointed him again.

A lump formed in her throat. She lifted her chin and struggled to swallow.

Then, as soon as she was able, she spoke. "Like I said before, I've just been trying to tell you about Amanda. Are you finally ready to listen?"

Chapter Five

Trent didn't want to be alone with Jolene. And he had made it his number one goal to stay away from moms. Single mothers sought stability—and he was not up for anything remotely resembling that. He made a living on the back of a bull, after all.

And, well, no offense to Jolene, but one day—in the distant future—when he was ready for a relationship, he'd settle down with someone who had class. Someone people respected.

Someone nice.

Trent thought about that some more. What he wanted was a nice girl. Yeah. That's right. What he was going to want was a lady.

Not a woman half the men in the town knew too well.

Knowing he was in that group of know-it-alls didn't help his peace of mind none, either.

Jolene's past—and his part in it—did mean he needed to treat her with respect. His dad would expect that much. So would his conscience. Looking at her closer, seeing the longing in her eyes, brought him back to their past. Back to when he'd first realized that he had so much and she had so little.

"Jo, if it's money you need…"

"I don't want a handout."

He bit his lip, steeling his resolve. He felt bad for her situation, and also a little irritated with her, too, for putting him in this position. He wanted to help her, but he also wanted some time to process what she'd just sprung on him. He wanted to take her to the door and tell her that he'd see her later. But the last thing he wanted to do was hurt her feelings.

Fact was, she made him nervous. All of a sudden, he couldn't help but recall just how well those lips had fit on his. Just how well they'd parted for him. How sweet she'd tasted.

How, for just a second, he'd felt tender toward her.

But he'd been drunk.

Since he was sober now, he needed to remember that Jolene was in his past. She was a nice woman, but she was never going to be much more than a gal on the trashy side.

Their paths really didn't need to cross again. Ever.

At least, that's what he'd planned on. He was a man who liked things being exactly what they seemed. These new developments with Jolene? Well, they were making him crazy, and that was a fact.

She was still standing there in that snug red sweater, looking like a cornered hen just hours before a Sunday dinner. When their eyes met, her chin went up. "Don't you have anything to say, Trent?"

By now he'd forgotten what they were even talking about. Desperately, he tried to smooth her ruffled feathers. "Jolene, don't get all emotional, now."

She adjusted that ugly purse on her shoulder and picked up the baby in the carrier. "You haven't even seen emotional from me. Of course, I don't know if you'd even know what honest emotion was if it bit you in the butt."

That made him squirm. "I would. We were plenty emotional the night we got together."

"I'm surprised you even remember. We, uh, weren't at our best."

"No, we weren't." All that whiskey had bypassed his empty stomach and gone straight to his head. But because he wasn't proud of his behavior, and because she was acting so snippy—he struck back. "I don't suppose it mattered all that much to you anyway, Jo. I mean, I was just one of many men rolling on your carpet, right?"

Fire flickered in her eyes. "Trent Riddell, comments like that show you don't know anything. *At all.*" And before he could open his mouth to defend himself, she walked out of the room and through the front door.

He managed to get it together, and followed her outside.

A burst of wind greeted them both. The sky was dark and the vehicle she was walking to looked like it had seen better days in 1989. "Hey, Jo, let me give you a couple of hundred," he said, pulling out his money clip.

She paused as she buckled the baby's carrier in. "I don't need charity."

"It's not a handout. Consider it payment for…" His voice drifted off. He couldn't really think of anything to say.

"For sleeping with you?" She slammed Amanda Rose's door, surprising a startled cry from the baby. "That would have to mean that what we did together was good, Trent. And believe me, it was hardly worth a nickel." She drawled out her last words as she looked him up and down. "I've had better sex from men double your age."

Double?

He was still trying to come up with a sharp retort when she drove out of sight.

DRIVE. INHALE. EXHALE. Brake at stop sign.

As Amanda Rose cooed and jabbered in her carrier, Jolene did her best to concentrate on what she had to do. Did her best to concentrate on getting them back to their apartment in one piece. At the moment, she didn't know if that was going to be possible because her hands were shaking uncontrollably.

Jolene was sure there were dozens of times she'd been more embarrassed, but she sure couldn't remember when.

Trent Riddell had looked at her as if she was no better than the burst of snow that had blown in with her when she'd arrived. Maybe "no better" wasn't an apt description. Maybe it was fair to say he didn't have any feelings for her. At all.

She'd been mortified. So mortified that she found herself being glad that Amanda wasn't old enough to realize that her mother was being judged and found wanting.

Oh, that look on his face!

Around her, snow swirled and blew pretty designs in the night sky. The patterns reminded her of one of those geometric screen savers on the computer she used to have. If you blinked, the pattern changed and morphed into something entirely different.

That was kind of how she felt at the moment. She'd realized that Trent Riddell thought of her in a completely different way than she thought of herself. She imagined herself fairly organized and a survivor.

He thought of her as white trash.

She'd imagined that though they'd slept together after a few shots of Jack, their long history and friendship would have been brought to the forefront again. He'd remember that underneath all that eyeliner, she was a nice person. A person who was trying to do her best.

A person he was once friends with. A person his whole family had been friends with.

He, obviously, only viewed her as some kind of easy floozy. And a mistake. A big mistake.

Of course, Trent was right. Seeing him in that big house with the marble and the woodwork and the leather couches in the living room, she'd been all the more aware of her status. Of her look in gray slacks and boots and thrift-store coat.

And of how different she must look from the women he probably dated. When, you know, he wasn't catting around in honky-tonks.

The women he took out to dinner probably wore gold watches and had facials and manicures. Their sweaters probably came from Neiman Marcus. Their boots from Lucchese.

Twenty minutes later, she pulled into her parking place and shook her head in dismay at her sweet baby. Of course Amanda Rose was now sound asleep. A ride in the car never failed to do that to her. Jolene knew the moment that they entered the apartment little Amanda was going to open her eyes and start fussing. Just when her momma needed to settle down after her tangle with Trent Jerkface Riddell.

She'd just unhooked the carrier, locked her car and

swung her purse on her shoulder when one of her neighbors called out.

"Jo, is that you?"

Addison Thomas. She struggled to keep her voice even. "Yep."

Before she could think of anything more to say, he was trotting over. "What's going on?"

"Nothing much. I'm just getting home."

He reached out to help her carry Amanda. With a bit of reluctance, she let him. Her biceps would appreciate the break, even though a part of her hated to give up her baby's care. Ever.

"Home from where?"

No way was she going to tell him about the disastrous meeting with Trent. "Nowhere special."

"Oh. I've just been working out." He grinned.

"That sounds like fun." She fought to smile as they walked side by side through the dark, snowy parking lot. Addison was not exactly all brawn. Actually, he was more along the lines of lean and stringy. With a bit of belly flab built in.

"It wasn't fun at all. Did I tell you I started working with a personal trainer? He's kicking my butt."

"I thought that was the point."

"Maybe...maybe not."

Now they made it to her door. "You can just set Amanda Rose down, Addison. I'll get her inside."

"I've got time. I'll wait until you unlock your door."

She was getting uncomfortable. "All right," she said slowly. She dug a hand in her purse and fished around for her keys. And then fished some more. Finally, when she located the key and slid it into the lock, a good two minutes had passed.

To her dismay, he turned the knob and walked right inside. She flicked on the light behind him. "Well, thanks again."

After carefully setting the still sleeping baby down, he turned to her. "So, since you're not doing anything now, how about we visit for a while?"

"I don't think so. I'm pretty tired."

"You're not ready for bed, are you? It's only nine."

The innocent question was accompanied by a look of wanting. "No. But I am ready to just sit. Thanks again, Addison. I'll see you around."

Instead of stepping toward the door, he leaned back against the white paint of the wall. "You look sad. How about some company?"

"No thanks. I'm not in a very good mood. I wouldn't be much of a conversationalist."

"We wouldn't have to talk, Jo."

So, that was where his kindness had been leading. Why was she even surprised?

Oh, but her hand ached to slap him. But they were neighbors. And that was her reputation. The good-time girl. So she laughed him off. "Good night, Addison."

Surprise knotted his brows. "You're serious, huh?"

"I am. Good night."

"Well, sure. 'Night, Jo."

The moment he walked through her doorway, she closed the door with a snap and dead bolted it. Oh, he made her want to take a shower!

As Amanda Rose slept on, Jolene went to go do just that. Maybe the hot water flowing over her shoulders would relax the knots that had suddenly appeared there.

Maybe all her worries would disappear down the shower drain, too.

She had bills and a baby and a reputation in ruins.

And only about another month's worth of money in her checking account.

And very few options.

Moments later, she learned that even the cleansing water of her shower did no good. No matter where she went, her problems seemed to be glued to her. No amount of soap was going to wash them off.

Tears soon mixed in with the spray. And then her knees went weak.

Before she knew it, Jolene was sitting on the cold, hard tile, crying her eyes out. And a very sweet baby sat silent, watching her on the other side of the glass.

Chapter Six

"So, I was thinking you and me were overdue for a little heart to heart," his dad said late that night.

Trent set down the tumbler of Jim Beam he'd been nursing for the past hour and shifted uncomfortably as his dad took a seat across from him. "I figured as much."

Balancing his elbows on his knees, his dad pierced him with a gaze. "Tell me more about you and Jolene. And Amanda."

"I don't know much more than you."

"I don't agree." His father's eyes hardened. "I think you've been might busy, son."

Trent felt his cheeks heat as the lump in his throat grew. "Jo and me got a little carried away one night. That's all."

"And you didn't use protection."

"No."

"What did you say?"

The tone told Trent everything he needed to know. "No, sir," he amended.

"So everything is really all your responsibility, isn't it?"

"I swear, I didn't know she was pregnant. I didn't know about Amanda."

"Because you didn't see the need to treat her right. Did you?"

"Dammit, Dad. It was just a one-night thing—" Trent took a breath as he tried to come up with the words to describe what life had been like out on the road. All a lot of women wanted from him was one night.

But before he could continue, his dad held up a hand. "That sorry explanation is your problem, Trent. You shouldn't have been treating women like that…"

"Dad…"

"And especially not Jolene."

The statement shamed him. But pride made him keep talking. "You know, nothing's certain. We don't know for certain that I'm the father."

"Oh, I think plenty is certain. You've just told me that you treated Jolene disrespectfully, were too full of yourself to be a man and check up on her, and now still don't want to accept responsibility. You've shamed me, son."

Trent felt lower than a rattler's belly. "Yes, sir."

"You listen to me, and you listen well. You need to make things right. Pronto."

"Yes, sir."

"I'm glad we talked." After a moment's pause, his father slapped his hands on his thighs. "All right now. Here's what we're going to do. I'm to take Ginny to Florida so you can get your act together."

"There's no need to leave."

"Oh, there is. You've got a mess to clean up and a woman and a baby to get to know. I don't want your sister witnessing that."

"Honestly, Dad…"

"Listen to me, son. There comes a time in every

man's life when he has to decide he's done being an idiot. This is your time. Start making decisions based on what is best for Amanda and Jolene instead of just you." With a sigh, he got to his feet and started toward the door. "It's time to grow up, Trent. You best do that and make your mother proud."

When he was alone in the living room, Trent leaned back and thought about everything he'd done and everything he'd put off. And then he thought about his mother, and the way she'd always smiled at him when she hugged him good-night—as though she'd thought he was something special.

It was time he deserved that look again.

"TRENT, HOW YOU HEALIN' up?" Steve Zimmer boomed on the other end of the cell phone.

"I'm getting there," Trent replied as he maneuvered his truck down the bumpy road to the west barn. Continuing to hold the steering wheel with one hand and his cell with the other, he wondered why his agent had decided to give him a call. "What's going on?"

"I was just thinking about you. A couple of sponsors have let me know that they're going to be checking out the Silver Tour in Rapid City. Think you can make it?"

The Black Hills Stock Show was in February. "I don't know."

"That's the wrong answer, Trent. We need you. The sport needs you, too. You're turning into something of an attraction."

"It's probably just 'cause that bout with Diablo got posted on YouTube." Shaking his head, Trent cursed the anonymous fool who had decided to tape Diablo stomping on him, zooming in on his grimace of pain, and then posting the whole damn thing on the World Wide Web. All in record time.

"That YouTube segment's been a regular little diamond mine, that's true. But your blue eyes don't hurt none, either, Trent. Girls are swooning every time they see that close-up of you getting your butt kicked." He paused. "So what do you say?"

"I can't commit to any tour dates yet, Steve. I'm stuck here at the ranch for a while."

"What do you mean, 'a while'?"

"I don't know. My brothers are out of town and my dad's recovering from heart surgery. And my sister, well, she needs me right now, too." Not to mention all the things with Jolene that had to be worked out. "I need to hold down the fort."

"No one else could do that?"

"I don't think so. Plus, my arm still ain't a hundred percent."

"I hate to hear that, Trent. I've got to tell these sponsors something. They'll bide their time for a bit, but not forever. If you don't get back in the ring real soon, your career is going to be over."

Over. That's what he was afraid of. He was afraid he was going to finally break something bad enough to send him to the hospital for a month next time.

And fear wasn't good. "I'm not in prime condition," he muttered as he parked his truck and climbed down out of the cab. "If you want to know the truth, February sounds too early."

"Aw, man…"

"It's true, Steve. I haven't been on a horse since I got home, never mind a bull." Plus, he had no desire to get on one, either.

Just realizing that made him cringe.

Steve paused again, then turned his voice sweet. "Maybe you should see one of those sports psychologists or something…"

"Maybe." But more likely, maybe not. "Listen, Steve, it's good of you to call, but I've got to go."

"You can't give me another five minutes? I'm trying to manage your career here."

"I know it. And I appreciate it, I do. I'll call you soon. 'Bye," he added in a rush before he clicked off and strode to the barn.

Now that he was off the phone, he was more aware than ever of the elements—and of how weak he'd become. Growing up, there were days when his dad would have all three of them outside in the cold and snow for hours at a time. Whining and complaining only earned him a cuff from one of his older brothers.

And it never made the work go away.

Now, though, every burst of wind was burrowing into his bones like a weevil. Making his body hurt and his muscles scream in frustration. Worse than all that, his bones weren't healing as quickly as he'd like. And there wasn't a thing he could do about that except to bide his time.

Bide his time before he lost all the endorsements that he'd worked so hard to achieve. And that were so scarce in his chosen profession.

Still ruminating about Steve's call, Trent unlocked the padlock on the door and pulled it open. At first look, everything was as it should be, but then one of the inventory books flashed into his head and he recalled the many items that Jarred had listed. Balers and cultivators and spreaders. Power saws and snow blowers. All kinds of expensive equipment that a ranch like theirs needed to have on hand.

Where was it all?

The air was musty and stale. He kept the doors wide-open, not even caring about the cold seeping back into his muscles as he walked around the space. Looking behind bales, he half hoped he was going to find a loose odd or end.

Or maybe a two-thousand-dollar power saw.

There was nothing there.

A truck pulled up just as he was circling around the area like the dumb cowboy he was, hoping that farm equipment was suddenly going to appear out of nowhere. Trent strode toward the front just as Pete, one of their longtime hands, entered the building.

"Hey, Trent," he said.

"Pete." He nodded and tried not to notice that Pete was looking at him under the bill of his cap as though he was a visitor. The complete opposite of how the guy greeted his brothers. With Cal and Jarred, Pete was respectful.

With Trent, Pete acted as if *his* family owned the outfit, and Trent was just wandering around, getting in the way.

"Do you need something?" Pete asked, pulling a piece of straw from a bale and popping it in between his teeth.

Uh, yeah. He needed all the equipment. For a second he was tempted to ask, but then he thought the better of it. If the answer was obvious—that it had been moved to another barn—it would prove to Pete that he was even less qualified to be there than everyone already thought.

But if the items were gone, it meant someone had taken the equipment, and that someone was counting on him not finding out about it.

The best thing to do would be to play his cards close to the vest. At least for a little bit.

"Nah, Pete. I'm good. I just thought I'd look around."

Pete was older than him. Older than Jarred, in fact. His prematurely gray hair matched the silver in his eyes. And seemed to accentuate his permanent tan.

That, at the moment, looked a bit lighter than usual. "Trent, I can take you around if you want. Give you a tour."

"I don't need that."

"I don't mind." He grinned. "Shoot, I'm sure you've got better things to do than traipse through here in the snow."

The man's manner grated on him. For a moment, Trent was tempted to put the guy in his place. Tell him that he wasn't as green as the guy obviously thought.

But the instinct that allowed him to gauge a bull's disposition in a heartbeat kicked in and told him to play the dumb cowboy card for a while longer.

"Don't you worry about me none, Pete," he replied, in an almost exaggerated, good-ol'-boy drawl. "Like I said, I was just taking a little ride. I'm going to head on home and rest my arm for a while, anyhow."

"Can I get you anything?"

"I'm good. I'll lock up now and be on my way."

For a moment, Pete looked as if he was stuck in a mud hole with no way to turn. Then he nodded and followed Trent out.

When Trent was locking the padlock, he glanced Pete's way. "How many people have these keys, Pete?"

"What?"

Trent held up the keys and jiggled them a little.

"I'm not rightly sure," Pete said, finally pulling the straw from his teeth. "Probably your brothers and father do."

"I mean besides family...any idea?"

"I couldn't say exactly."

"Maybe we should check into that, hmm? You know, just to be on the safe side and all."

"Oh, sure. Sure."

As the flakes started falling again, Trent gazed at the sky and grimaced. "Don't think we're going to see a lick of sunshine anytime soon. Wouldn't you say?"

"What? Ah, no."

"Well, you keep warm now. I'll see you later, Pete."

The hand visibly relaxed. "Sure, Trent. See ya."

As Trent opened his door, he called out. "Hey, Pete? Come to think of it...what brought you out this way?"

"I'm sorry?"

"I read the schedule this morning, and I could have sworn I saw that you boys were going to be inoculating cows near the north barn. What brought you out this way all alone?"

After a deer in the headlight moment, Pete turned cocky. "I'm just trying to do my job, Trent. We all know you ain't used to things around here. I'm just doing my best to make sure you don't get hurt."

"That's real kind of you." Jackass.

Pete winked as he climbed in the cab. "It was no problem. No problem at all."

Now, that's where that man was mistaken, Trent decided. There was something very wrong going on.

And before everyone came home again, he was going to get to the bottom of it.

He might be a rodeo star, but he was also a Riddell.

And no matter what everyone else thought, that name still meant something to him. It meant security and land and a heritage.

It meant oil and horses and brothers.

It meant his dad. It meant little Ginny, and the promises each one of them had made to their mother on her deathbed.

In short, the name Riddell still meant a lot.

Maybe, right at that moment, it meant more to him than ever before.

Chapter Seven

No matter how mixed-up things might be, no matter how screwed up her life was, there was a fact that trumped everything else in Jolene Arnold's life.

Amanda Rose, her beautiful little bundle of joy, was a Riddell.

And that, well, that was something pretty darn special.

Yep, even at three months of age, little Amanda was headed toward a better future than Jolene had ever dreamed about.

Being a Riddell meant security and respect. Being a Riddell meant opportunity and choices—all things Jolene had had precious little of but used to yearn for like other kids yearned for chocolate ice cream.

But until Jolene could figure out how to get Trent to do anything but schedule a paternity test, all of her big hopes and dreams for Amanda needed to be put on the back shelf for a while.

Because she needed to get back to work.

With a sigh, Jolene put on her "uniform," such as it was. Bob, the owner of Bronco Bob's Honky-Tonk, didn't care too much about what she wore, as long as she could meander through the tables and serve drinks and smiles without a lot of fuss.

Some women wore T-shirts and jeans. But Jolene had learned that a little cleavage worked wonders in the tip department—and those tips made the difference between a box of mac and cheese and baked chicken for dinner. Without even looking in the mirror, she slipped on her jean short-shorts, a black tank top—low enough to show a discreet bit of black lace—and her boots.

This little getup was going to be cold as heck on the way to Bob's, but she'd be warm enough once she was working hard. Bob's furnace ran two ways: hot and hotter.

She'd just swiped lipstick across her bottom lip when her best friend Cheryl knocked, right on time.

"How are you doing, sugar?" she asked, her auburn curls looking tamed for once.

"I'm fixin' to go to work," Jolene said with a grin. "Again."

"Looks to me like you're working that body of yours."

"Yeah, well, a girl's got to do what she can with what she's given..."

"But you've been given so much." Cheryl shook her head in exasperation as she poked Jolene's tummy. "Girl, when are you ever going to look like you had yourself a baby three months ago?"

"Hopefully not anytime soon. I've got bills to pay."

"It's just not fair that you look that good in a tank and shorts. I still looked like a beached whale eight months after Tyler was born. You, on the other hand, even looked sexy when you were six months along."

She might have looked sexy at six months, but

definitely not after that. A lot of the men had taken to ignoring her, either feeling bad asking a pregnant girl for beer, or maybe just not eager to look at a woman who was so swollen with baby.

Soon after, Bob had asked her to help Carter in the back of the bar, but that had been a courtesy job. Carter hadn't liked the idea of her being on her feet all night long. The most he ever let her do was wash glasses and fill snack jars.

She'd practically lived on mac and cheese then.

"As long as the boys tip me, I'll be fine."

"I'm sure you'll be more than fine tonight." Once more looking over her figure with a hint of jealousy, Cheryl sighed. "Now, don't forget to save me some stories. You know how I like hearing about your antics."

"I won't forget."

What Jolene didn't say, though, was that she wouldn't have minded Cheryl sharing some stories about her life, too. But of course that would just be embarrassing.

Cheryl was happily married, and living Jolene's dream. She had Dwayne at home, who thought Cheryl had done something pretty darn remarkable by growing a baby in her stomach. Dwayne wouldn't have cared if Cheryl had gained a hundred pounds, he was so smitten.

But things were a fair sight different for Jolene. She'd learned to rely on herself the best way she knew how. It was up to Jolene to bring home the bacon or she'd have nothing to cook. And, well, no one had ever made a secret of enjoying anything other than her sassy smile and curvy figure.

As Cheryl took off her fleece coat, mittens and scarf, Jolene picked up her bag. "Amanda Rose is still taking her nap. I expect her up within the hour." Glancing at her watch, she winced. "I'm late again. But…do you need anything?"

Cheryl waved a hand. "I'm fine. Go on, now."

"I've got a bottle in the fridge, and some chips and wine if you want some."

"Don't worry." She winked. "Dwayne is going to bring me some dinner on his way home from work."

"Enjoy that for both of us, will you?" Jolene's mouth watered. Dwayne worked at the Golden Dove and Cheryl was always talking about the latest dish he was trying out.

"I'll do my best. Now go on, honey, before you're late. Don't you worry about Amanda or me none."

She took two steps closer to the door. "Have I thanked you properly for sitting for me twice a week?"

"There's nothing to thank me for. My mamma's enjoying grandma time with Tyler, and my husband's bringing me dinner. All I have to do is sit here, hold Miss Amanda, then watch TV and nap until you come home. Believe me, being here's a real treat."

"Thank you—"

"Go, Jo."

With a brief wave behind her back, Jolene grabbed her ski jacket then ran out the door.

And wished she was sitting next to a roaring fire, sipping tea and watching *Frosty the Snowman* instead of almost turning into one.

Bob's was loud and bright and booming when she slipped in the back door. Carter, one of Bob's bartenders, was sitting in the storage room having a cigarette.

"Oh, Carter, you're gonna get in big trouble," she teased as she walked past his perch and pulled off her ski jacket. "You know Bob don't like us smoking back here."

Before answering, Carter lit the end of a new cigarette with the remains of his first one. "Bob's just going to have to deal, Jo. It's freezing outside. No way am I sitting in the alley."

Looking at the goose bumps on her legs, Jolene nodded. "Don't I know it. I thought my rear end was going to freeze to the seat of my car before I made it here."

Carter shook his head as he exhaled. "That would be a shame, given the caliber of your butt...but it would also be your own fault." He looked her over and shook his head. "A girl needs to know when to put on more clothes, and that's a fact."

"You know the guys like seeing me in this."

"You could change when you get here."

"Carter, that would take more time than I ever give myself. Don't fuss. I'm fine."

"All I'm saying is that you've got to take care of yourself."

After pulling out her short canvas apron and tying it neatly around her waist, she shrugged. "This girl also needs to eat, Carter. I'll see you out front."

She left just as she heard the rustle of another cigarette getting pulled out of its pack. Feeling better about quitting smoking, she shook her head at poor Carter. He was going to die of lung cancer before he was fifty at the rate he was going.

Jolene was still thinking about Carter and his nicotine habit when she entered the noisy front room. At least a dozen people surrounded the bar, some chatting in groups of twos and threes, others looked happy to just be taking up a bar stool.

Surrounding the bar were too many tables, each one filled. Karaoke was going on. Bruce Barnes was singing an old Brooks and Dunn Christmas standard, as off-key and mournful as ever. Popcorn was on the tables, peanut shells on the floor.

It was also smoky and loud and hot as hell.

Immediately, her tank seemed to become glued to her skin.

Just like any other night. Since it was crowded, she smoothed things down a bit just to make sure her girls would get the attention of all the boys in the room.

"Jo! You're here."

"Bob, I'm sorry I'm a bit late," she said as she approached. "Where do you want me?"

"Well, Sarah and Marnie have this room just fine, so I need you out in the game room. Ginger could use a hand, I'm thinking."

She gritted her teeth. "I'll get right to it." There was no denying it—she hated the game room. It took forever to get back and forth from there to the bar.

The poor economy had induced a ripple effect at Bob's. Men out of work came in for a quick morale boost, which led to a surge in business.

Which led to Bob's greatest idea…a grown-up game room. After expanding the place—and giving a much needed financial boost to a local remodeling company—he bought a couple of old pinball machines, a jukebox and a secondhand pool table.

Now it was a regular hangout. Smoky, loud and filled with the constant barrage of dings, loud Bon Jovi singles and a crew of men who were wanting to relive the eighties.

It only took a moment to find Ginger. "Oh, I'm so glad you're here!" she exclaimed, a bit out of breath as she headed toward the bar, balancing a six-pack of empty beer bottles on her tray. "The men are thirsty tonight."

"That's great."

Ginger nodded. "It's good for my pocketbook, hard on my back."

Pasting a smile on her face, she entered the room. Immediately, she spied the usual suspects. Andrew, the grade school principal was sitting with his wife and another couple. Two mechanics were sipping and dippin'.

George, from over at the Electra Lodge Retirement Home, was having his weekly glass of Scotch with his old neighbors.

And then there was Trent Riddell.

Damn.

"Hey, Jo?" one of the mechanics called out. "Do we gotta ask you out before you serve us?"

"Heck, no. I'd never go out with you, Casey," she teased as she sauntered over and took his order.

A few other people ordered beers. George called her over to say hey. She pulled out a pencil and pad and wrote everything down and ran back and forth from the bar, delivering beer and shots of Jim Beam and smiles and sass.

As she'd hoped, either the Christmas spirit or her skintight top was doing the job. Tips were coming in strong, and not just a buck or two, either. When a pair of college boys from Tech gave her an extra twenty…if she promised to slide it in her back pocket, she complied with a laugh and smile. No one was doing much besides a little flirting and she did so love getting that cash.

All the while, Trent watched her. Making her wish suddenly that her shorts were a little longer and her top was a bit more modest. Or, well…at least that he wasn't watching her get those tips.

His scowl was disconcerting. So was his glare.

When she passed Ginger in the tiny hallway outside the game room, she leaned close. "Ginger, take care of Trent Riddell for me tonight, would you?"

"Sure?" She winked. "I thought y'all had a history."

"Oh, we do. But I don't want to talk to him tonight."

Compassion filled the other server's eyes. "Sure, then. Don't worry, Jo. I'll deal with Trent. You won't have to go near him if you don't want to."

With that piece of business taken care of, the night flew by. Over and over, she and Ginger crossed paths while they took orders, collected beer bottles, passed out beer tabs and playfully flirted. Ginger kept her word and visited with Trent often. Jolene took care to not look his way.

Until 1:00 a.m. when he called her over.

Chapter Eight

The temperature in the already warm room rose another ten degrees as Jolene took a deep breath, adjusted her tank top yet again and walked on over to Trent.

He made no secret that he was watching her. Blue eyes lit on her boobs and slowly slid upward, apparently enjoying the view.

And dammit, her body responded in kind, getting all heated and tingly and eager for his touch. That, of course, she completely resented.

"Hey, Trent," she said. "How're you doing?"

"Not so good, if you want to know the truth," he drawled. "I've been sitting here all by myself. All night long. Watching you avoid me." A line formed between his eyebrows as he glanced at his arm—which was encased in a yellow Oxford shirt with not even a hint of a wrinkle. "Just like I've got leprosy or something." Shifting, he crossed one scuffed roper over a stretched out leg. "Honestly, Jolene, were you really goin' to try to ignore me all night?"

Try had been the key word. Because, well, she had been *trying* to ignore him. Trying really hard. But trying to ignore Trent was like trying to ignore the oil spill in the Gulf—it was impossible to do.

"I'm not ignoring you, Trent. It's just been real busy in here."

He looked around. "Yeah. I can see that."

Of course, the place was half-empty. A little line of sweat started making its way down her back as she tried for normalcy. "Now that I'm standing here in front of you, why don't you tell me what you want. What can I get you?"

"You."

She just about choked. "Say again?"

Trent scowled. "Shoot. You know what I meant. I want to talk to you. Sit for a while, Jo."

"I can't sit down. I'm on the clock. Working," she added.

"Don't you get breaks?"

"Not this close to closing. It's almost 2:00 a.m., you know." She shifted her weight on her left hip and lifted her chin, trying not to glare at him.

What the heck was he doing, asking if she wanted to sit with him and chat? How come he hadn't been that nice and friendly when she'd been at his fancy house with Amanda? "What do you want to drink, Trent? What can I bring you?"

"Club soda."

"No beer?"

"Like you said, it's getting late. I'm going to need to drive home—sooner or later." His voice lowered as the brim of his Stetson lowered a bit, too. "So, darlin'... how about you get me a club soda?"

If she got any more hot and bothered, she was gonna need to be doused in a tub of ice.

"I'll be right back," she murmured, then turned and walked to the bar before she changed her mind and decided to sit with him. As she waited for his order, all she could do was wonder about why he'd called her over to him.

Was it something as simple as he just wanted to say hey? Or did he want to apologize again for insulting her?

Her footsteps slowed. Or...did he have something else in mind? Something that had to do with hook ups... and things that they'd done before?

Her mouth went dry and her skin went cold—a fairly remarkable thing, given that it was about a billion degrees in the bar.

Shoot. What if that really was what he had in mind? Just another night with her—just another night of meaningless sex.

Carter delivered Trent's club soda, and with a smile, she took the glass and returned to Trent, realizing as she did so that now they were the only two people in the game room.

The brim of his hat was tilted low as he watched her enter. She didn't know how he did it—it was most likely some skill he perfected on the circuit or something—but his blue eyes sparkled like diamonds. Or, um, sapphires.

Blue diamonds?

Something exotic and foreign and special.

And, just like always, she felt her whole body tense up and tingle as she stepped forward. "Well, here you go. One club soda."

"Sit with me?"

She'd run out of excuses not to. And frankly, it would seem a bit strange if she didn't sit next to him. Sitting with men was what she did. And the rest of the room was now empty.

She sat.

Trent sipped slowly, swallowing a good fourth of the liquid in one gulp.

"You were thirsty."

"Always."

"I've never been one for club soda, but watching you, maybe I'll—"

"How's Amanda Rose?" he interrupted.

Jolene looked at him curiously. "She's good."

"Who's she home with?"

"My friend Cheryl. She comes over and naps on the couch when I work nights."

"And…she's a good friend? You trust her?"

"She is. I pay her, of course, but she lets me off cheap. I'm lucky to have a friend like that."

"You think it's safe, leaving Amanda at home with a woman while you're here…working?"

"What else am I supposed to do with her? Bring her here?"

"Of course not." He looked mildly embarrassed. "Just, I don't know. It seems to me that a baby needs to be home with her mother."

"This mother is working."

"At a bar."

She took exception to his glare. "I've made over two hundred dollars tonight. Where else do you think I can make money like that?"

"Hell. I don't know…"

"This is a good job. Bob treats me well. Carter does, too. They're good people."

Trent sipped again, draining the glass. "I'm just saying that maybe you should be worrying about your daughter more."

"I'm providing for her."

"Like this."

Jolene felt her cheeks heat, but she wasn't sure if it was from embarrassment or anger. Both were pretty much fighting for first position in her brain. "Trent, just what is it about me that you find so awful?"

"Huh?"

"I told you that this is a good job. I told you that I'm making good money and have her in a safe place. But here you are, acting like I'm still dirt under your boot."

"I've never given you that impression." That propped boot settled back on the ground.

"It feels that way. It feels like even though you got me pregnant, I'm the sole floozy here."

"Jeez, Jo." He looked around to his left and right and winced. "Stop saying that. We haven't even gotten the blood work done yet."

She snapped her fingers. "Gosh, I plumb forgot. I guess we'll have to keep waiting a little longer to figure out how Amanda mysteriously got Riddell eyes."

He winced. "Do we really need to broadcast that?"

She lowered her voice. "If I was broadcasting, I'd tell everyone that we did it on my living room floor—that we were so hot and bothered, we couldn't even find time for a bed."

His eyes flashed. "We found one. Eventually."

"Ah, so you do remember." She batted her eyelashes. "Did you also remember that you didn't use a rubber?"

Even in the dim light, it was obvious he was blushing like a seventh grader on a pool deck. "Jeez."

"But who's listening, anyway? And who would really be surprised, even if they did decide to eavesdrop? You sleep with everyone."

"And you don't?"

Anger. Yes, that was exactly what she felt. Burning hot and fierce inside her. "Not anymore," she bit out.

"Not since me?" Pure surprise lit his eyes.

Which so did not make her feel better.

"That's right. Not since you, Trent." And not since she'd realized she was pregnant.

And not since she'd realized that even Trent—a guy who she'd once followed around like a puppy dog, a guy who she used to sit on the school bus with, wasn't afraid to dodge her phone calls.

No, he hadn't returned a single one of her phone calls when she'd tried to tell him the news. Because she'd been forgotten.

Stung again by the memory, she stood. "Now that we've discussed my babysitting options and your concerns about them—all without volunteering to help in any way, mind you—may I get you another club soda?"

With a jerk, he shook his head.

She pivoted on her heel and left him there, fuming. As she walked out of the game room, she spied Bob leaning against the wall, watching her approach.

His face was blank, but to Jolene, he might as well have had a billboard hanging from his nose that said he'd been listening to every word.

Tucking her chin to her chest, she attempted to scurry by.

His hand on her arm stopped her in her tracks. "Jolene?"

She raised her head. "Yes, sir?"

"Why don't you call it a night?"

"It's not two yet."

"It's close enough. It's been a good night, and you

worked your tail off. Go collect your money and get on home," he said quietly.

Oh, no. Was she getting fired? "Bob, I'm sorry. I didn't mean to piss off Trent—"

"Oh, honey. You don't need to apologize. I'm not upset." He grimaced. "Not with you, anyway. But it's late. Head on home. And make sure Carter walks you out."

"I'll be fine—"

"Ask Carter for help." His voice brooked no disagreement.

She slumped. "Sure. I'll do that."

Walking toward the bar, she saw Carter was already standing in front of it. He was holding an envelope, too. "I've got your tips," he said, handing her the money. "Go get your coat. I'll wait for you here."

Looking at her buddy, she noticed that his expression was pinched and his voice was rougher than usual. "Carter?" she asked hesitantly. "Am I in trouble or something?"

"Hell, no. Bob, uh, has just had enough of Trent Riddell for a while. That's all. We all have."

Though she hadn't thought it could be possible, Jolene felt her spirits sink even lower. Well, great. It seemed that everyone she worked with had heard her little conversation with Trent.

And not a one of them was happy about it.

Chapter Nine

After giving up on seeing Jolene again, Trent was just slipping on his sheepskin coat when Bob pulled up a chair. "Hey, Bob. I was just headin' out."

"Why don't you rest your feet for another minute or two?"

Bob had a whole new thread of steel in his voice, which kind of took Trent off guard. "All right. Anything you want to talk about?"

"As a matter of fact, yes." Bob took a seat and crossed his arms over his barrel-shaped chest. "How about we talk about Jolene?"

Worry and wariness slammed into him. "What about her?"

"I'm a little partial to the girl, Trent."

Whoa. Quickly, Trent schooled his expression so that he wouldn't look as appalled as he felt. But shoot! He was shocked. He had no idea Bob had set his sights on her. After all, Bob was old enough to be Jo's father. "I see."

Bob slammed a hand on the table, causing Trent to jump. "No, you don't. I'm not after that girl." He scowled. "Honestly, Trent. Can't you ever think of anything other than what's in your pants?"

"Since I'm still recovering from getting the crap stomped out of me by a bull named Diablo, obviously, I can."

But instead of grinning like most folks did when Trent told his stories, Bob just glared. "I think that bull should have stomped your brain instead of your arm. Or maybe he should have aimed for your buckle."

Even the image of a bull's hoof heading toward his, uh, privates, made him squirm and shudder. And get defensive. "What the heck is that supposed to mean?"

"It means, Trent, that I overheard what you said to Jolene." He paused. "And what she said to you. Tell me something, is that baby really yours?"

"That is none of your business."

"I'm thinking it might be."

"Why? Because she works for you?"

"Because she's my friend."

Trent was about to say that Jolene was his friend, too, but Bob kept talking. "Jolene is a good woman, Trent. A lot of men get sidetracked by her looks, but I'm telling you what, she uses it to her advantage like no other. She's a hard worker, and she's smart. She makes a pretty decent living here. More than just about anyone else."

"I'd never dispute that. I know she works hard."

Folding his hands on the table, Bob sent him a level look. "Jolene hasn't had an easy time of it. It's been hard for her, raising that baby on her own."

"I'm sure it has been difficult." Trent was tempted to say more; but what could he say? It was a shame that Jolene was a single mother and making her living in a bar. But it wasn't his fault, 'cause he hadn't known about Amanda until a few days ago.

Bob's eyes narrowed. "I'm going to tell you a story."

He was trapped in hell. "Please don't."

"You know, my wife was the shyest, plainest looking wallflower you ever did see when we were in high school. One day we ran into each other on the way home from school. I was still all hopped up on my touchdown from Friday night's game…and she was walking along, carrying her flute case like it weighed a thousand pounds. I decided to carry it for her, thinking she'd be starstruck."

Against his will, Trent was sucked in. "And?"

For just a second, Bob's craggy face lost his pissed off expression and became all googly-eyed. "And, she put me in my place, Trent. She said, 'Bob, one day you're going to realize that there's more to me than frizzy hair and glasses.'"

Lord, save him from 2:00 a.m. conversations! "You've lost me."

Bob cracked his knuckles. "Obviously. What I'm trying to tell you, Trent, is that there's more to Jolene than a near-perfect ass and a beautiful face. One day you need to realize that."

"I do."

"Good. So don't sit and glare at her anymore in my place of business. I don't like that."

"All right. I'll do my best not to." Whatever that meant. He was so confused by the whole situation, he didn't even know what he was supposed to be doing any longer.

As if they'd just decided something earth-shattering, Bob heaved a sigh. "Well, it's closing time, and I, for one, am about ready to call it a night." He looked him over. "You okay to drive?"

"Yeah. I only had two beers, and that was an hour ago."

"All right then." Now that the hard stuff was over, Bob stood and looked almost cordial. "Well, now, have a good night, and be careful getting on home. And thanks for coming in."

"Sure thing, Bob. 'Bye," he added as he walked outside and paused for a long moment, letting the cold wind cool his face and clear his head.

He strode over to his truck in time to see Jolene's little sedan pull out of the parking lot.

Moments later, as he pumped the clutch and started the ignition, Trent looked out into the distance and saw nothing but stars and shadows on the horizon.

He thought about him and Jolene, back when they were small and still neighbors. And how innocent and pretty and sweet she'd been.

So eager for a kind word. So eager to be included.

And he felt ashamed. He needed to do more for her. A whole lot more.

Chapter Ten

The next morning, he was making Ginny eggs and giving them both a pep talk. "Today's a new day, sugar, which means you've got to have a plan to make it a good one."

Ginny, sitting on a bar stool in jeans, a sweatshirt with a horse on it, and cowboy boots, looked skeptical. "I'll try, but something always happens."

Out of the mouths of babes. "That's what I'm talkin' about," he retorted. "It's when things go bad that you've got to dig in deep and try a little harder to be good."

"Hitting Peter wasn't good, but it wasn't all bad, Trent. Sometimes he really deserves it."

Scooping out the eggs onto a plate, he tried to deal with little-girl logic. "But we don't hit. We've already covered that one."

"I know." She picked up her fork when he set the plate in front of her. Then she looked at his empty place mat in confusion. "Where's your breakfast?"

"I ate hours ago." Actually, he'd been so worked up from seeing Jolene and getting a talking-to from Bob, that he'd made himself an omelet and a slew of bacon when he'd rolled in a little before three.

After that, he'd gotten four hours' sleep, then got

up to take care of Ginny because he couldn't stand the thought of her going off to school in the cold with just a bowl of cereal in her belly.

Sipping his coffee, he watched her eat. "Taste good?"

"Uh-huh. Almost as good as Jarred's."

"Thanks."

Around a mouth full of buttered toast, she said, "Daddy said you're a daddy now, too."

He choked on his coffee. "He told you that?"

"Well, no...I overheard him talking to Junior on the phone." Tilting her chin up, she whispered, "Are you really a daddy?"

He nodded. "I might be. There's some tests to be taken. I'm waiting to see if they say I'm the baby's daddy." But even as he said it, Trent knew the truth in his gut. He'd fathered that baby.

"If they say so, what are you going to do?"

"Be a daddy, I guess." He blinked in surprise. For the first time, being a daddy didn't seem all that bad.

"Where's the baby? Is it in Wyoming?"

"Wyoming? Why would you think that?"

She shrugged. "Junior and Jarred said you like girls everywhere. I thought maybe the baby lived somewhere else, too."

That shamed him. Especially since, well, he'd had enough buckle bunnies sharing his bed to have a collection of offspring that he didn't know about. "The baby lives here. Her name is Amanda Rose. Ain't that pretty?"

She nodded. "Can I see her when Daddy and me get back from going to Florida?"

The reminder that his father was taking Ginny away

because of him made Trent feel about two feet tall. "Maybe. I'll have to see what her momma says."

Luckily, Gwen showed up at the kitchen door before Ginny could go into full cross-examination mode. "Time to go to school, Virginia."

"Okay." After sliding off the stool, she ran to the mudroom to get on her coat and backpack.

Trent looked appreciatively at the woman who did so much to keep the household running. "Thanks for taking her, Gwen."

"It's no problem, Trent. It's what I do," the older woman said as she turned around and started shuttling Ginny out the door.

When the kitchen was empty, Trent rinsed off the plate and thought about what he and his sister had talked about. Things like accepting responsibilities and doing things one didn't necessarily want to do.

With that in mind, he knew it was time to follow some of his own advice, even if it didn't go over well.

JOLENE HAD HER HANDS FULL of wet baby when the doorbell rang. After wrapping the towel around Amanda a little more securely, she opened the door. Then stood stock still as Trent came waltzing through—as though he visited every day.

With barely a flick of his wrist, he pushed the door closed behind him. Turning to her, he scowled. "It's freezing outside. What are you doing, carrying that wet baby to the door?"

"It's nice to see you, too. Why don't you make yourself at home? Oh, yeah, I forgot. You already have." And with that, she turned around and walked back to the bathroom. At the moment, she couldn't care less about why Trent was standing in her apartment. All that really mattered was that she needed to get Amanda dried off and warm.

But of course he couldn't help but follow. Leaning against the door frame, he watched her place Amanda back down on the bathmat and put her feet into the pink terry cloth pajamas. "Oh, Jo. Look at her tiny feet."

She spared him a look. Then, noticing that he was falling in love right before her eyes, motioned him over. "She's cute, isn't she?"

"She is."

Though his tone, so soft and full of awe, made her feel more than a little squidgy inside, Jolene resolutely kept her attention on her daughter. Solely on her daughter. It was a fact—Trent Riddell was starting to drive her crazy.

He cleared his throat. "I'm sorry I snapped at you when I came over. I shouldn't have been so critical."

"No, you shouldn't have. You have no idea what it's like, raising a baby by yourself."

He flinched. "We both know that's true, don't we?"

The thread of disappointment in his voice made her realize what she'd said—and also realize that she hadn't intentionally set out to hurt his feelings. "I didn't mean for that to come out as it did. Sorry. Was there a reason you came over?"

"As a matter of fact, yes." Trent put the seat down on the toilet and sat down, as if that was the best seat in the house. "After we talked at Bob's, I started thinking things over. About your babysitting situation."

It was difficult, but she kept their conversation on target. It wouldn't do to start getting all soft where he was concerned. "Okay…"

"I'll get to it," he muttered.

She glanced up at him.

There he was, staring at Amanda Rose. Transfixed.

Exactly the way she knew he would be, if he'd ever taken the time to get to know her.

"She is just adorable."

"I'm fond of her, that's for sure." Jolene grinned as she finished snapping up Amanda's outfit, though it was a hard task. Her little angel was rolling around on the floor.

Peering at Trent again, Jolene decided to let him win. She was too tired and stressed to beat up on him anyway. And too grateful for another adult to watch over Amanda for a moment. "Would you like to hold her while I clean up all the towels and toys?"

Automatically, his one good arm reached out. His other one, out of the brace for a while, hooked out at an angle. "You don't mind?"

"Not at all." Feeling a little shy, she muttered the obvious. "I mean, she is your daughter, too. I'd be grateful for your extra pair of hands."

His lips curved. "Or hand."

Liking his little joke, she tenderly handed Amanda off. "If you took her into the living room, I could get this bathroom cleaned up in record time."

"Will do." Trent wrapped his arms around the baby as if she was a prized possession—which, of course, she was.

Then, without hardly a backward glance, he got to cooing, stood up and walked right out the door. Amanda, that tiny traitor, didn't give a single whine of resistance.

"Her blanket and stuffed toys are on the floor next to the couch," she called out.

"I see them. Take your time."

Yet another bout of nervousness surged forth. Jolene couldn't help but smile at the sight of the two of them together. One day they were going to have to really iron things out. And she would have to figure out what, exactly, she wanted from him.

But for now, she was just going to be happy he was there to watch the baby while she put away the small bottles of baby shampoo and body wash, drained the tub and gathered up the old diaper and towels.

Maybe she took a little longer than she needed to. Maybe it really was a pleasure to take the time to put everything neatly away and to start a load of laundry.

But finally, when she could no longer put it off, Jolene joined Trent and the baby in the living room. "Thanks for holding her," she said, reaching out to take Amanda Rose back.

"It was my pleasure," he said, making googly eyes at the baby and keeping her securely in his arms. "Hey, do you mind if I hold her a bit longer?"

She was okay with having a mommy break, but suddenly she felt as though she was missing an appendage.

And feeling more curious than ever about his appearance. "Trent, why did you stop by?"

"I wanted to talk to you about your job."

"We've already discussed my job. I told you that I'm tired of you acting like it's not good enough."

He swallowed. If he was hurt by her surly conversation, he didn't show it. "I decided that maybe we should sort some things out between us."

"What things?"

"Like…maybe we should move forward."

If Jolene had ever thought her heart could stop beating from emotional pain, this moment was the time for it to happen. "How do you propose to do that?"

"Spend some time together."

"Just in case, when we finally take those tests, you discover I'm not a liar." A slow, sinking feeling hit her hard as she realized yet again that Trent Riddell may be handsome as all get out, and a champion bull rider, and even her childhood pal…but he could also be a royal jerk.

Little by little, some of his confidence looked to be slipping. "You're…you're upset, aren't you?"

"That you don't believe me?" She shrugged. "Sure I am, but that won't make the reality any different. When you schedule the tests, let me know."

"I'm only doing this so I can do right by you if I am the father."

"Oh, Trent. Financial obligation is the least of it." Walking toward the door, she curved her palm around the handle. "Well, now that we've gotten that taken care of…"

"Listen, I was also thinking that I'd like to spend some time with her. Sometimes."

"What?"

"It's my right, don't you think? And you could use the help. You know. When you're working." He avoided her gaze as if he was embarrassed.

Which kinda made her like him a little bit better. Steeling herself, she said quietly, "I'm not so sure that would be a good idea."

"And why is that?"

"Because you're going to be going soon." When

he frowned, she explained. "You know…going on the road."

"So?"

"So, you'd hardly get to know her before you'd be gone again." Suddenly, Jolene felt as if all the air in the room had been sucked out. "You know, we could have done this on the phone. Why didn't you call about this?"

"I didn't want you to hang up on me."

"I would have, too."

"I know I'm making a mess of this. Listen, when do you work on Monday?"

"Two to eight."

"That early?"

"I don't just serve beer at Bob's. I help him with his paperwork and taxes, too."

Something flickered in his eyes. "You really do know how to do all that, don't you?"

"Like I told you before, I'm good at a lot of things."

"How about you come over for a bit before you go to work, and then I could watch Amanda when you're gone."

"Really?"

"I'll do my best." Trent grinned as Amanda grabbed hold of one of his fingers and squeezed experimentally. "She's got a good little grip."

Once again, Amanda was serving as their bond. They had so much garbage between them, only Amanda could cut through all of that and make them make an effort. "She's a girl who knows what she wants."

"No shame in that, I suppose."

"How much time do you need?"

"Probably more than you could give me…"

He glanced her way, and the tension rose between them, making her flash back to when they were naked.

Unable to stop the pain that rushed forward, she turned away.

He noticed. "Jo, why don't you just tell me everything you were going to say the other day."

Right. Like she wanted to feel as though he was skinning her all over again. "Why are you being like this? Why are you suddenly interested in still knowing me and Amanda?"

"Because maybe I am."

"I don't have time to get dressed up and show up at the ranch again. If you want to see what I've got, you're going to have to see it right here."

Trent blinked as her words hit the space in between them. As that familiar sense of attraction sparked again.

"I can do that," he replied.

Shoot. Was his voice huskier than it had been?

"Then put Amanda down on her blanket and come over here to my desk."

After a moment's hesitation, he followed her.

Jolene opened up the photo album on her desk and pushed it toward him. "I thought you might like to see what you've missed," she said softly.

Trent's expression was blank as he stared at Amanda's baby pictures. But, little by little, Jolene saw emotions flicker in his eyes. When he glanced at a picture of a tinier Amanda, he brushed a finger across the photo. "How old is she here, Jo?"

"Three weeks."

He turned to her, his lips half turned up. "She's bald."

Jo laughed. "She was, but she soon got that pretty hair of hers."

"She was still pretty, though." His voice sounded a bit hoarse.

"I thought so."

For a good long moment, they stared at each other. Then Trent broke the connection. With a shake of his head, he turned away and crossed the room. When his arm brushed the corner of the couch, he winced.

"Your arm is still paining you, isn't it?"

"Yep, but it's no big deal."

She couldn't help it, she reached out to him. "Trent—"

The muscle under her hand hardened. "I'm fine, Jo."

With a bit of insight, Jolene realized that he was probably used to saying that. Used to covering up his problems with some swagger and a sly smile.

Even when he wasn't fine at all.

"Be careful on the sidewalks. Some are icy."

"I'll do my best."

"And I'll call you later."

"I'll be waiting. 'Bye, now."

After he let himself out and closed the door behind him, Jolene watched him hobble down a step and to his truck. All with a minimum of fuss.

And that's when she began to understand that it was very likely that both of them had grown up a lot over the years. She was still impulsive. So was he.

But each of them had also begun to realize that there was more to the other than they'd originally thought. Maybe it was age. Maybe it was responsibilities—she had Amanda Rose, and he had the ranch. Or maybe it was just life.

Life always did have a way of pushing dreams aside and forcing reality to be front and center. For better or worse.

Chapter Eleven

Trent's cell phone rang as he was pulling into the front gate of the ranch. With one hand he answered, with the other, he pushed the electric gate opener on the visor.

"Trent, here."

"Hey. It's Cal."

"Junior, how are things? Y'all enjoying your vacation?"

"We are. We're loving Walt Disney World. Matter of fact, I even told Susan we should look into getting a time-share here."

"Really?"

"Uh-huh. After all, it is the place where dreams come true…and our family is expanding."

"Is Susan pregnant?"

"No, but I hear you're a father."

When the gate opened all the way, Trent drove through, then pulled over to the side. "So that's why you called."

"Well, it's pretty big news. How are you doing?"

It was on the tip of his tongue to say he was just great, but that was a lie on so many levels he didn't think he could do it. "Truthfully? I don't know."

Junior paused. "Do you know what you're going to do?"

"About what?"

"About Jolene. About the baby. About your rodeo-ing…"

"There's not much I can do. After the paternity test confirms that everything's like Jolene says, I'll figure out how to help with the baby."

"Dad says the baby has your eyes."

"That's true, but a lot of people have blue eyes." He cleared his throat, hating the way his macho pride was getting in the way of what his gut was telling him was right. "Anyway, there's no reason to talk about this now."

"You sure? 'Cause Dad also told me he and Ginny are heading our way tonight."

"That's true." Trent frowned again.

"What happened? Why are they coming out?"

"Dad's hoping I get my act together." He paused. "Actually, I think he's so frustrated with me that he doesn't want to be around me right now." Trent winced. No, it was more like he'd been a huge disappointment. And darn if it didn't still hurt. "We can talk about it when y'all get home."

"Okay."

Shoot. Now that was a surprise. He'd been sure he was about to get the third degree all over again.

After a second's hesitation, Cal said, "How's every-thing else going? Are you having any trouble with the computer or any of the ranch business?"

Trent leaned his head back and felt yet another layer of his worth slide down further. Was that how his broth-ers thought of him? That he just went around riding bulls and couldn't handle anything else? "I'm tackling the ranch business okay. I'm having a little bit of trouble with the financial stuff, but Jolene's actually going to come over and help me out."

"I didn't mean to offend. It's just that I know handling everything by yourself must be difficult."

Trent rolled his eyes. He'd heard that condescending tone all his life. He was old enough to know Cal didn't mean anything by it—he really was sincere about wanting to help.

But Trent knew that if he let on that he had questions about everything, his brother would know he not only couldn't handle his love life, but he wasn't too good at dealing with the ranch either.

But he could handle it. And as far as the finances, well, he still couldn't figure out Cal's complicated filing system. And he still had no idea about what, exactly, he was supposed to ask their financial advisor when he met with him next week. Then there were the concerns about overtime for the hands. And the empty barn that was supposed to house all their farm equipment.

But if he gave into temptation and started asking questions, his brother was going to feel as if, yet again, his younger brother couldn't do a damn thing right.

So he lied. "Everything's fine."

"You sure?" Cal didn't even try to hide the surprise in his voice. "Because I have time now to sit with you and walk you through some of my usual routines on the computer."

Slowly, he drove toward the house. "I'm not even in the office right now. I'm just comin' back from town."

"At 10:00 a.m.? What were you getting? Inoculations? Are we low on antibiotics?"

Trent hadn't even known he was supposed to be monitoring any of that. "I was out seeing Jolene. Not that you're thrilled about that."

Trent parked the truck and turned off the ignition. 'Cause he knew that wasn't exactly true. Cal was cordial with Jo, but he'd drawn a steady, invisible line between them, and their station in life.

"I don't have anything against Jolene personally." On the other side of the line, Cal paused, clearly choosing his words with care. "You need to provide for your baby, not involve her mother in the family business. It's just that history doesn't mean a thing when it comes to financial success, Trent. I thought you understood that."

There Cal went again. Talking to him as if he was dumber than a prairie dog. "I understand more than you might imagine."

"Now, don't get all bent out of shape—"

Trent was so fired up, he got out of the warmth of the vehicle and stood outside, letting the frigid air fan his cheeks.

When he finally had his temper in check, he replied. "You might think I've been doing nothing but pocketing my winnings, but I actually have been investing it. And I haven't lost it all yet."

"Now, see here. I'm not sayin' a thing against you. It's the baby we're talking about."

"No. I think it's far more than that." Suddenly, protective instincts he didn't even know he possessed rushed forward. "Jolene is a good person, and she's as honest as the day is long. I think she's going to be just the person I need to help me make heads and tails of everything, and keep things on track."

He kept his voice firm, daring his brother to spout off about Jolene again.

But finally that voice must have registered because Cal cleared his throat. "Well, okay, then. I was just checking in. Is there anything you need to speak with Jarred about? Everything going okay with the hands?"

Well, there was the little matter of Pete and the missing inventory. But at the moment, Trent was in no hurry to get on that parade. From the way his middle brother was speaking to him, there was a good chance that his oldest was going to turn the missing equipment into his fault.

Looking out into the distance, at frost decorating every fence post, at the pair of pines next to Ginny's swing, at the barn door in need of a new coat of white paint, he repeated. "Everything's fine."

"Sure? 'Cause I know I would have had a question about—"

"I'm positive," he interrupted. "Now, y'all have a good time and I'll call you if I need anything. You don't need to call again."

There was dead silence on the line before his brother cleared his throat. "Trent, I'm sorry about what I said about Jolene," Cal said after a moment. "Mom would have chased me with her wooden spoon if she'd heard me speaking like that about Jo. It was unkind, and just plain mean. That girl never could catch a break."

"Accepted."

"Maybe it's a good thing, you two ending up like you are..."

"We're not ending up together. We just happen to be parents together." Remembering that they still had to take that test, he coughed. "Maybe."

Heading toward the house, he made a new plan. They'd work together and get stuff done. And when they parted ways again…when he went back to the circuit and she went back to her life, they'd both be able to look back on this time together fondly. And he'd never again feel that twinge of regret that crept up in the middle of the night.

Then he remembered that he'd slept with her and moved on. And had never even considered picking up the phone when she'd called.

Chapter Twelve

On Monday morning, the wind was blowing hard enough to make Jolene's trek to her car seem longer than ever. It took all her strength to balance Amanda's carrier with one hand because she was holding a worthless umbrella in the other.

Actually, Jolene didn't know why she was bothering to shield herself from the sleeting rain. In the space of one minute, the wet gusts had managed to undo a full hour of fussing in front of the mirror. Now her hair was a mess of wet hairspray and tangles. She'd be lucky to comb through it, let alone put herself to rights again before she got to work.

As another gust of wind threatened to pull the umbrella from her hands, she stopped and closed it with a sigh.

Stuffing it in her tote, she picked up Amanda again and trotted to her car.

"Jolene? Jolene, stop, would you? Let me give you a hand."

With a start, Jo saw Addison striding her way, looking as successful and debonair as ever in a silver hat, black leather ropers and black barn jacket.

He grabbed a hold of Amanda's carrier before she

could do more than smile a hello. "Addison, this isn't necessary…"

"Sure it is. You're going to be soaked to the skin if you're not careful. Now, hand me your keys, would you?" He held out his left hand.

Since she needed help anyway, Jo handed the keys to him as another gust of wind blew on through and pulled at the tails of her wool coat.

As she wrapped it more securely around her middle, Addison unlocked the driver's side door, turned on the ignition and then proceeded to clip Amanda's car seat into the back.

"Thanks," she said grudgingly.

"No problem." While the car ran and the heater warmed up, he popped open his umbrella and looked at her kindly. "You know, I wish you'd call me when you have your hands full like this. We're neighbors, Jolene. I never mind helping you out."

His words were kind. Gentlemanly. So why were they so hard to accept? "I wouldn't want to be a bother," she murmured. And, well, it wasn't likely she was ever going to start calling him when she was carrying the baby to the car. Addison looked at her as though she was needy and he was her knight in shining armor.

Unfortunately, she'd never been into all that. It was easier just to take care of herself.

"You wouldn't be a bother," he said. "Just keep me in mind, 'kay?"

Instead of acknowledging that, she took a step back. "Well, this wind and rain isn't helping my appearance none, so I'm gonna get going."

"Where are you heading in such a hurry?"

"To the Riddells'."

"Really?" His eyes narrowed. "I didn't think you were close to them."

His words were innocent, but they grated on her all the same. There was an undercurrent of innuendo that she shouldn't know the Riddells, that they were out of her league. "I've known them for years," she said. "And I really should be on my way."

As quickly as she could, she got in the car, which was thankfully warm, since he'd turned the heat up high. "Thanks again for your help, Addison."

One strong hand clasped her door and held it, so she couldn't pull it toward her, even if she wanted to. "Call me when you need help. Promise?"

"I promise," she said sweetly, knowing that in truth she was only going to call him if she was desperate. "Look, I really need to go. This sleet is going to make the roads bad. I don't want to be late." Pasting on one of her smiles, she tugged on her door. "'Bye, now."

He held up a hand as she closed her door, but his parting look was pure speculation.

As she carefully shifted the car into Drive, Jolene shook her head in dismay. One day she was going to have to set Addison's mind straight. She wasn't going to win any awards for church choir behaviors, but even at her worst she wasn't who Addison Thomas seemed to think she was. A weak woman who needed someone to save her.

Jolene was still stewing on their conversation, and that look in Addison's eyes, when she drove under the very fine arch leading into the Riddell Ranch. Through the slush that had attached to her windshield wipers, she noticed that someone had hung two wreaths on the fence posts, bringing a welcome burst of color to the gray December day.

Five minutes later, she was walking through the back kitchen door with Amanda's diaper bag on a shoulder and the carrier in her other hand. When she'd called inside, Trent poked his head out. He was on the phone, but motioned her on in.

After she shut the door, he called out, "Go get yourself some coffee, Jo. I've got to gather a couple of things real quick before I forget to do it."

Looking around the large, magazine-pretty kitchen, all painted in a sunny golden-yellow, Jolene set Amanda's diaper bag and carrier down. "Well, this place looks like sunshine, doesn't it?" she murmured as she pulled off her jacket and tried to fluff up her wet, soggy hair.

Amanda, still snug in her spot, yawned and looked around with interest. "We're gonna have a real good day, sweetheart," she said, pulling off the thick blanket covering the baby.

Amanda replied by kicking her feet.

Pushing worries about her appearance aside, Jolene smiled as she followed her nose to the pot of freshly brewed coffee. Standing next to the pot was a container of cream and an oversize ceramic mug.

Smiling at Trent's thoughtfulness, Jolene glanced around and wondered where she was going to work. Then, with Addison's words still fresh on her mind, she began to have a good share of doubts.

What if Trent was simply expecting the same thing Addison thought she was offering? What if all that hemming and hawing about finances and paperwork and getting to know Amanda had been just talk?

The thought made her sick to her stomach. More than

ever, she was glad she was doing good enough on her own. Never again did she want to have to depend on a man for her success or happiness.

"Trent?" she called out again. "How about you just tell me where you want me to be?" As soon as she said the words, she felt her cheeks heat. *Shoot.* Could anything sound more suggestive?

"How 'bout you set up shop right there in the kitchen?" he said. "And I promise I'll be right there, I'm just running a little late this morning. One of the horses was favoring a leg. Checking her out took me a bit longer than expected."

"She okay?"

"She's fine. Had a rock wedged near her shoe," he replied, still sounding distracted. "Just relax for a sec, now, would you?"

"All right." Feeling a bit restless, she wandered to the desk. On top was a calendar with all kinds of appointments neatly written in. Near the beginning of December, it looked like Trent's sister, Ginny, had been a busy girl. Choir and play practices were noted and checked off, along with class parties and one trip to Amarillo.

Putting her finger on the neat printing, Jolene wondered who took care of all the planning and errands. She'd bet a dollar it wasn't Mr. Riddell. Maybe Cal?

Maybe Jarred? Or his new wife, Serena?

"What are you looking at?"

Startled, Jo turned on her heel. "What? Oh, nothing. I was just wondering who took your little sister to all her activities."

His arms full of a plastic crate, he looked at her

quizzically. "I was going to do a lot of it…until Dad decided to take Ginny to Florida. Why?"

"Oh, I don't know. I guess I was just thinking that all that running around takes a lot of time." And that one day she was going to have to be running around with Amanda.

His features relaxed as he walked over to the large kitchen table and set down the box. "Dad tells me that most of the arranging is my brothers' doing."

"Not your dad?"

"Heck no. He loves our girl, but if we left the raising of Ginny to him, that girl would be hanging out at the barn all day. And playing poker."

"That's sweet," she mused.

"It's disturbing, that's what it is." He crossed the kitchen and refilled his mug. "It is. She loves her daddy. But, in some ways, I think my brothers do more in raising her than my dad does. Jarred and Cal have patience to spare, and give her attention, too. And know when to get her in line, too."

Jolene noticed he didn't mention himself.

Thinking of the little girl's busy schedule, she said, "I'm surprised you all let her do so much."

"I'm glad we keep her busy. Cal and Jarred tell me otherwise she's a real handful."

"I'm sure she's going to appreciate everything y'all have done."

"I'm afraid I can't take any credit for Ginny. I'm usually gone, you know," he added with a frown.

In a sudden burst of insight, Jolene realized that Trent wasn't real happy about that. She had always assumed he was happiest on the road. Maybe not?

"Hmm." Pushing away her own memories, she

smiled at Amanda. "No telling what my baby girl is going to be into."

He looked at the baby fondly. "Time will tell, I guess?"

As she looked into his blue eyes, she felt her heart melt yet again. With effort, she brought up the sore spot for both of them. "So...did you figure out who to call about the test?"

He looked down at his shoes. "I did. Dr. Williams said all he needs is some blood from me and Amanda, then he turns the whole kit into some fancy lab that specializes in those types of tests."

"Did you make an appointment for us all to get tested?"

"No. I thought I'd talk to you first." He cleared his throat. "When would you like to do it?"

She didn't want to do it at all. "Probably the sooner the better."

"Tomorrow or Friday?"

"Either's fine," she said, struggling to keep her voice nice and easy. "Now, how about I start helping you with some of that work?"

"Sure you don't mind?"

"I don't mind." When he still looked uneasy, she stepped next to the table and picked up a folder. "What's all this?"

"Files about the different accounts and stock holdings. A lot is on the computer, but I have a heck of a time reading through pages of notes on an electronic screen. I thought you might feel the same way."

"I do. I'll take a seat and read through these things. Or do you want me somewhere else?"

He blinked. "Jo? You're sounding almost nervous. You okay?"

"Of course."

"Sure? You seem rattled." His eyes narrowed as he looked her over some more. "Are you having second thoughts about me watching Amanda?"

"I'm not having second thoughts."

"All right…" His voice drifted off as he glanced at the baby. "Is it me? Are you worried that I'm not going to treat her well? Because if that's what's on your mind, I promise that you don't have a thing to—"

"It's not you…"

A lone muscle in his jaw quivered. "Is it me? Are you worried that I'm not going to treat you right?" he asked in a rush. "Because if that's what's on your mind, I promise, you don't have a thing to—"

"It's not you, Trent." Then, because his manner was so sweet and she was so grateful that he actually had only been thinking about *working* with her, she murmured, "I had a conversation this morning that set me off, if you want to know the truth." She shook her head, already feeling dumb about even bringing it up to him. "It's nothing."

But the concern that immediately flared into his eyes didn't look like nothing. Actually, it looked like he cared. "What happened?"

"Oh, it was nothing. Just one of my neighbors. He kind of likes me. He…he was helping me to my car and he just said something that didn't set well."

"What did he say?"

"Nothing you need to worry about." There was no way she was going to bring anything Addison had said to Trent's ears. She was on shaky enough ground as it was.

"Who was it?"

"Trent, it was nobody you'd know."

"Probably not. So why don't you tell me?" Leaning back on his chair, he crossed his arms over his chest. "You know, if you don't tell me, you'll practically be a liar, because we promised each other that we were friends, you know."

"We are."

"So if you're holding out on me, things don't look real promising for our new emerging friendship…"

"Addison Thomas," she finally admitted, just to shut him up.

At the mention of Addison's name, Trent looked at her curiously. "I know Addison. What did he say?"

"Nothing important. He just gave me the impression that you and I probably shouldn't have too much going on between us."

"Why is that?"

"I don't know," she lied. Not wanting to admit that in the scheme of things, some facts couldn't be changed. Trent was a famous, wealthy rodeo star from a wealthy family. She was not.

They'd made a baby together, but that didn't mean jack in the eyes of most people.

"You know, maybe I should visit with him. You know, set him straight about our relationship."

"There's no need. I did that." Oh, this was a nightmare. Trent Riddell on the path toward righteousness was scary to watch. And, dammit, kind of mesmerizing.

Actually, to see him getting all hot and bothered about her honor was taking her breath away, too.

Jumping to her feet, she said, "Hey, would you mind if I went outside and got Amanda's Pack 'N Play and set it up in here?"

"Of course not, but I'll go get it."

"There's no need—"

He matched her tone. "Jo, I'm gonna help you. So just accept that as a fact and move on. Is your car unlocked?"

She nodded.

"Then I'll be right back."

The minute he left, she sat down and exhaled. Oh, but she needed to get a hold of herself and fast! Being around Trent was messing with her head.

When he returned, together they set up the Pack 'N Play. Then after Amanda was happily lying down in the middle of it, chewing on her squeaky worm, he met her gaze.

"So, are you ready?"

"I am. I've got more than enough to do."

"Okay. Well, then…I'm going to make a couple of phone calls," Trent mumbled.

"I'll make us a better cup of coffee, too."

"If you can do that, you're already a huge help."

"I can do that. I can do a whole lot more than that," she murmured as he walked away. "All you had to do was really look at me and listen."

Chapter Thirteen

By lunchtime, he'd come to the conclusion that Jolene was just as hard of a worker at his kitchen table as she was serving beer over at Bob's bar. That girl didn't seem to believe in breaks.

At first, he'd occupied himself with ranch business. He worked in his father's old study, catching up on correspondence.

When that got old, he went out to check on the horses. After seeing that they were just fine, he returned to the house and settled in across from Jolene. While Amanda napped and Jo examined files and entered material on her laptop, he read stock reports.

And then tried his best to start tracking down all the inventory that he'd thought was in the barn but hadn't found when Pete had wandered in.

But all the while, he couldn't help but watch Jolene. He looked for signs that the day was getting too long for her. But that had been unnecessary. The woman had no trouble holding Amanda and typing on the computer at the same time.

Or feeding her a bottle while examining the contents of a file folder. In fact, she really hardly looked to be needing anything from him, which was a surprise.

But then he couldn't stand it anymore and started asking questions. "Tell me about being pregnant."

She laughed. "Not much to tell. I was big with a baby."

"Come on. I really do want to know. What was it like? Were you sick? Did you crave ice cream? Pickles?"

After looking at him a little bit longer, a dreamy expression settled on her face. "It was good. I liked being pregnant." She curved her arms around her middle, as though remembering what it had felt like to be carrying another life inside her. Almost shyly, she added, "Amanda loved to wiggle around eight at night. I used to lay flat on my back and watch my tummy shift."

Mesmerized, he leaned closer. "Did it hurt when it shifted?"

"Not at all. It was my favorite part of the day. Like having a baby was 'real.'" She shook her head. "Eight o'clock is still her busy time of day."

"And labor and delivery? It went all right?" He couldn't believe he was asking all these questions—he should have been there! But in spite of that knowledge, he couldn't help himself, either.

"It went fine. My friend Cheryl was with me, and the doctor said it couldn't have gone smoother if I'd tried."

"But didn't it hurt?" He'd heard it was worse than getting thrown off a bull.

"I suppose. I don't really think about all that. Only when I saw Amanda Rose for the first time. That's when I knew it was all worth it."

All worth it. And he'd missed it all because he'd been too busy remembering how many women wanted him... What an ass he'd been.

"So, are you sure you're ready to be alone with Amanda? I better get ready for work."

"I'll be fine."

"Since she just had her bottle she should sleep most of the time. I've left a bottle for her in case she wakes up."

"I'll be fine."

Picking up a tote bag, she headed toward the powder room. "Okay, then. Let me go change and then I'll be out of your hair."

It was then that he noticed she was planning on getting out of her jeans and sweater into two articles that were a whole lot smaller and tighter. "Shorts and a T-shirt again, huh?"

"Yep."

"Ever consider wearing jeans?"

"Only when I don't want to make much money," she said with a wink. "This is how it's done."

When she closed herself off into the other room, Trent winced, realizing she was probably right. When she was parading around in short shorts, it was almost impossible to not stare at her.

Jolene's problem was that she was just too pretty.

No, that wasn't it. Fact was, Jolene was *too much*. Too much for him, anyway. She was everything he'd ever liked in a woman, and then some. And then some more.

Jolene was a blonde—and boy howdy was she a natural blonde—and then those wide-set green eyes, so pretty with their flecks of gold, just made his knees go weak. And now he was coming to find out that she was smart, too. Real smart.

And a hard worker. 'Course, he had already known that.

"All righty. I'll call you when I'm on my way back."

He blinked. Gone was the mom who cooed at the baby. In her place was the woman who everyone thought was the true Jolene. She was gorgeous and stacked and made men think of things their wives wished they wouldn't. "You look good, Jo."

She winked. "I hope so. I've got my heart set on a new car."

"What do you want?"

"A van."

"No kidding?"

"Yep. I want one of those mommy-mobiles." She paused and bit her lip, almost as if she was embarrased. "Silly, ain't it."

"No…"

For a split second, Jolene stared at him, her lips parted slightly. And for that split second, Trent was dangerously close to leaning in and brushing his lips against hers.

And then crushing her to him and kissing her hard and deep.

That, of course, made him think of something else entirely—the two of them on her living room floor, naked and sweaty.

And that vision, dammit, made him realize that it had been a hell of a long time since he'd seen any of that kind of action. At least a month.

He stood up fast and stuck the kitchen chair in between them. Hoping against hope that it would cover up his rising uh, interest.

Pure embarrassment coursed through him as he

wished—once again—that he'd never been so desperate for help. That he'd never hired her at all.

When her tongue darted out, moistening that full bottom lip, Trent knew that something had to be done. A man could only take so much.

She looked at him long and hard, her eyes wary and her lips slightly parted. As if she wanted to trust him with all her heart—but she was afraid that he was going to turn on her like a mangy Rottweiler.

A deep sense of dismay filled him. Shoot—is that how she thought of him? As the kind of guy who would make promises and then drop them like a handful of hot potatoes?

Was that who he was? The air between them bristled with a new tension, one that had a whole lot less to do with sexual tension and a whole lot more to do with major disappointment.

A second passed. Two.

Finally Jolene pursed her lips. Another awkward moment passed as she digested that one. Then she nodded and pulled away from his touch. "Okay, then. I'll see you later."

Trent couldn't help but think that this could become a habit. And that, of course, scared him half to death.

Chapter Fourteen

Bob's was surprisingly busy when she arrived. "Jolene, you're gonna catch your death," Carter called out.

"Not me," she sassed right back with a smile. "Now, where do you want me, Bob?"

"Help out Carter, would you? The other girls can do the back room."

She didn't need to be asked twice. With the companionship that came from many, many hours of working side by side, Jo served drinks, commented on the shows on the television over the bar and chatted with some visitors taking a break on their way to Oklahoma.

As she'd hoped, customers were in a giving spirit. After ninety minutes, she'd gotten at least a hundred dollars in tips.

Then, as it sometimes did, they got a lull that gave her time to worry about Amanda—and about the man who was currently keeping time with her.

There was something simmering between her and Trent that wasn't altogether healthy. Well, at least not for her heart. All day long, she'd found herself looking at him when he wasn't noticing. Listening for his voice.

All that did was twist up her insides and make her wish for things that were never going to happen—like he'd suddenly wake up one day and fall in love with her. It also made her fantasize about things that shouldn't happen again—like having his tongue in her mouth and his body wrapped around hers.

"How many times have you called home, Jo?" Bob asked sometime after midnight when he stopped to check receipts.

"Not once."

"I'm impressed. Though, I guess Cheryl's used to the princess's whims."

"Actually, Trent's watching Amanda today."

"Is there a reason?"

"You do the math."

"He's finally stepping up, huh?"

"He is." Jolene was about to say more, but then she noticed he was sporting a satisfied grin. "What do you know that I don't?"

Bob—all two hundred fifty pounds of him—looked affronted. "Not a thing."

Remembering how he'd told her to leave early the other night, she took a stab. "Did you, by any chance, talk to Trent about me and Amanda?"

"Maybe."

"You didn't have to."

"I'm just looking out for you, that's all," he said gruffly. Looking her over, he asked, "So, how are things going over there, at the Riddell Ranch?"

"Pretty good."

His eyes narrowed. "You don't sound too sure about that."

"I'm sure. You know how that goes."

"Uh-huh."

She didn't blame Bob's skepticism—it was justified. Jolene knew that if she gave herself time to start thinking about all her mixed-up feelings for Trent, or how it felt to be near him all day, she was going to do something stupid—like tell Bob the complete cold, hard truth about her feelings for that cowboy.

Already it had been a shock to her system to watch Trent hold Amanda with such care. Almost as if he believed the baby was really his.

Bob cracked two knuckles as he looked at her fondly. "You know something, Jo? You're a good waitress. You show up on time, you're efficient and, hell, a lot of guys come in here just to look at your legs in those short shorts."

When she rolled her eyes, he chuckled. "In today's economy that can't be discounted." After a pause, he turned serious. "But more important than all that, I care about you. You're a good woman, Jolene Arnold. 'Bout time Trent realized that."

The compliments embarrassed her. Bob had never been one for saying sweet things. The only retort she had was to shrug off his words with a laugh and grin. As if the praise didn't feel like a soothing balm to her soul. "Oh, please—"

"I'm serious. Okay. Well, not about the men showing up to look at your legs," he corrected with a sly grin.

She lifted up one leg and flexed her foot. "I do have good legs," she joked. "Walking back and forth from your blasted game room can give a girl a lot of exercise."

Before she lost her nerve, Jolene went ahead and fished for information. "So…what do you think about Trent?"

"Other than he's one of the richest and most success-ful rodeo stars to come out of Texas?"

"Yes. I mean, what do you think about him as, you know, a person?"

"Trent's a decent sort," he said after a pause.

"That's the best you can do? Decent doesn't sound like much of an accolade."

"It's not. But it's probably all he deserves right now."

Well, that sounded cryptic. "What is that supposed to mean?"

Right in front of her, Bob clammed up. "Nothing."

"Bob…"

He held up a hand, pushing her off. "All you need to know is what you already know, Jo. Trent Riddell is trustworthy, and has a good heart. And, well, I think he has more inside him than he realizes."

Again, her craggy boss, who never failed to talk straight, was speaking in riddles. "Are you saying he's got potential?"

Bob laughed. "Uh-huh. The thing of it is, if Trent never did another thing his whole life, a lot of folks would say that was good enough. But that's not the kind of man he is, you know? He's the type to try harder. To push himself. To be more."

"I'm glad about that."

He leaned back against the hard wood of his chair. "So, how did today go? How did Amanda do with Trent?"

"She did okay." Thinking about her baby, Jo said, "I'm so lucky, Bob. She's such an easygoing sweetheart. She played on her Pack 'N Play, and didn't fuss unless she needed to be changed or fed."

"That don't surprise me none. She's been a doll since the day she arrived in this world. And how did you do… using your mind instead of your biceps?"

"Or my famous legs? I did okay, too," she said with some surprise. "I think Trent was kind of shocked that I knew what I was doing, if you want to know the truth."

"Good. You keep him curious."

"I think we're going to keep each other curious."

"And then what's going to happen with the two of you?"

"I guess we'll figure out how to raise Amanda together. Then, when Trent is healed up, he'll go back to rodeoing and I'll go back to asking Cheryl to help me out when I come into work."

"Good, 'cause as cute as Amanda Rose is, she's going to need to eat."

"Plan on me working New Year's Eve, okay?"

"I'll write you down on the schedule, but we'll play it by ear. Just in case, you know…maybe you won't end up needing to work so much. Or your plans change."

Getting to her feet, she stretched her arms over her head, working out the kinks in her back. "Tomorrow starts early. I better be on my way."

"All right. Good luck with Trent."

She still felt that pull toward Bob and her job, no matter how hard it was. Everyone at Bronco's had been so good to her, during her whole pregnancy, and even when she'd taken off a month to be with Amanda at home. "I'm off tomorrow, but I'll see you Friday night."

"Will do."

Impulsively, she hugged him. His big frame comforted her, made her feel small and slight. And his gentle hug made her feel cared for.

After a moment, he pulled away. "Let's not get all sappy, Jo. It's going to ruin my reputation. Now it's time for you to get on home. The weather's fixin' to turn."

Glancing out the window, Jolene saw the clouds had indeed darkened. Rain and sleet were on the way. "'Bye," she whispered, suddenly feeling as if she was saying goodbye to more than just Bob for the day. No, instead, it felt as if she was saying goodbye to her whole way of life.

She drove back to Trent's in a daze. "Everything go okay?" she asked the moment he let her inside.

"Considering I changed my first poopy diaper, I'd have to say it went well enough. She's fast asleep."

"Great. My car's still running. I'll just grab her and go."

For a moment, she was sure he looked disappointed. Then he lifted his chin and grinned. "How was your night?"

"Good. Good tips tonight."

"I bet." After yet another awkward moment, he spoke. "I…I heard from the doctor. All we have to do is stop by the office tomorrow and they'll take care of the rest."

"All right. Amanda and I will do that."

"Want to go together?"

"There's no need, Trent. I won't forget to go," she said softly, before turning away and lifting up Amanda.

"All right then, if that's what you want."

"It is."

"Call me in the morning," she replied, before turning around and rushing to the car.

She told herself she definitely was not looking forward to getting that test done tomorrow. Not one little bit.

Chapter Fifteen

On Wednesday, Jolene met Trent at the doctor's office. "I hope this doesn't take too long," she said, just to have something to say.

"I hope it doesn't, too." Looking at her sideways, he said, "My dad's pissed at me for doing this."

"Why?"

"You know why. He'd be tickled pink if you were part of the family. He's always had a soft spot for you."

"It's mutual. I've always had a soft spot for your dad."

"Jo, I know I've hurt your feelings, insisting on this test. I'm sorry for that."

She noticed he wasn't apologizing for the test. But she supposed she could handle that. Though she didn't need proof, she certainly had nothing to hide. And, if it eventually erased the last shadows of doubt in Trent's eyes, she'd do whatever it took.

She'd do anything for Amanda.

When the door opened, the nurse directed them to two separate rooms. "I'm going to take off after this, Trent. I'll see you at your house tomorrow."

As if he knew better than to press, he simply nodded and went to where the nurse directed. And she did the same.

The next day, after getting Amanda settled and making a fresh pot of coffee, she got to work. She started answering the phone more, and pulled the stack of bills from Trent's hands and began paying them online.

On Thursday, they visited a bit over a spreadsheet Cal had begun.

Little by little, Jolene got used to seeing Trent in a whole new way. Instead of simply thinking of him as the rodeo star, she began to notice that he had a serious work ethic.

And though she knew he could kiss like a dream and one smile could send her heart to beating double-time, Jolene was beginning to realize that he also was still the boy she'd known when they were little. He wasn't afraid to get dirty, and he wasn't afraid to get in the thick of things. He could be as scruffy and smelly as any cowhand after a morning's work in the barns.

And though everyone in town liked to say that God had spared Trent a whole lot in the brains department, Jolene was coming to find out that that wasn't true at all.

He'd taken to giving her to-do lists every morning before he left the house. The lists revealed a thoughtful mind. A man who took the well-being of the ranch's holdings as an extremely personal thing.

No matter what he said, he wasn't simply "doing his best" at managing the ranch. No, he was intent on running it. And running it well.

On Friday morning, when Jolene showed up with Amanda, she realized that things had taken a new turn.

"Morning," he said, meeting her at her car door.

"Good morning. What are you doing out here?"

"It's sleeting. I thought you might need some help."

"Trent, I can do this—"

"Say 'thank you,' Jo."

"Thank you," she said helplessly. But gratefully, too.

After he carried Amanda in through the icy rain, Jolene shrugged off her coat and laid it across a chair. Comforted by the warmth of the house and the smell of freshly brewed coffee, she sighed in contentment. Every day, this kitchen was feeling more like home.

"Now how about a cup of coffee?"

She turned to find him holding a mug, as if he was the star in a coffee commercial. "I'd love one."

"I'm going to pour you a cup. You tend to your daughter."

Half-afraid she was going to start getting used to being spoiled so much, Jolene sat down and got Amanda settled.

Only feeling a tiny twinge of unease at the mention of "her daughter." Would he ever feel that Amanda was his, too?

TRENT FIXED JOLENE A CUP of coffee while she did all those things with the baby that he was starting to learn came with the territory of motherhood. And all the while, Jo cuddled her close and murmured sweet things. All the things his momma used to say to him. And all the things they used to do for Ginny.

It made him nostalgic for how things used to be. "Until Amanda came over, I'd forgotten all about how many dishrags and cloths babies go through," he said, thinking out loud. "My sister, Ginny, spit up all the time. She was a real mess."

"I keep forgetting you boys practically raised your sister."

"Jarred and Cal did more than me. I was only sixteen when Mom died and only eighteen when Ginny was born. I'm afraid during her first year, I didn't do much more than play football and ride horses."

"That was to be expected. You were grieving, Trent."

He nodded. "It was hard. All I wanted to do was escape from this place for a while. That's what egged me on to work in the ring, and take risks with those bulls."

"Did it help your mind? Did things ease?"

"It did after a time. Slowly, I started appreciating things here. And, of course, I always did love my little sister. It was such a bad time for us, with her mom leaving and all, that Ginny gave all of us something to concentrate on." Thinking back, he remembered holding Ginny. Remembered her gummy smiles, and the way she'd called him Tent instead of Trent for a whole year—much to everyone's amusement.

Something new flared in Jolene's green eyes before she set Amanda down in her Pack 'N Play. "So, what are you working on today?"

He'd done quite a bit of thinking about projects that needed to be done, and he'd come up with inventory. Cal had done a good job of writing down every expense that was needed to take care of the ranch. Now it was definitely time to start trying to track down the missing items in the barn.

"I'm going to gather a list of items bought in the last four years, and how much was spent on them." Briefly he told her about Pete and his showing up at the barn on that Sunday. "Do you think I'm crazy for being concerned?"

"Not even a little bit." The line of her lips hardened. "Something's not right with that." Holding out her hands, she said, "How about I skim through the accounts?"

"You sure you don't mind?"

"It's why I'm here, right?" Jolene opened up her laptop, grabbed the flash drive she'd discovered the day before. And then, without another word, she started typing away.

For a second, Trent stood there, at a loss. A part of him had wanted her to need him, had half wanted Amanda to fuss and Jolene to look at him with a needy expression and ask for his help.

But of course, she didn't.

So he turned away, shrugged on a slicker, headed out to the barn and visited with a couple of hands. Maybe if he asked the right questions they'd give him more answers about what Pete was doing in his spare time.

Chapter Sixteen

What did it mean when she was disappointed that Trent was being nothing but considerate and professional? Jolene wondered about that later on in the afternoon, when, around one, Trent had shown up, his blond hair wet, his shirt sweaty, his cheeks pink from the cold. After washing his hands, they'd made sandwiches for lunch side by side. Then, after an apologetic look, he'd eaten his in his father's office. Not at the kitchen table with her.

Why had she been disappointed when he'd announced that he needed to make some phone calls, then go out with two of the hands for most of the afternoon?

Leaving her to enjoy that splendid peace and quiet of the Riddell home for a little while longer, she should have been happy to be trusted so much. And without him wandering around, she'd gotten some work done. Actually, she'd been able to find out a lot of information in her inventory investigation.

She'd found a whole variety of farm implements that were recently bought and they'd cost anywhere from a couple of hundred dollars to a couple of thousand.

Purchases like that added up. And it wasn't as though

they were diamonds or anything—they should all be in plain sight. She drummed her fingers on the table.

So if Trent hadn't been able to find them, who had taken them? And where?

Out the window, the sleet had turned to an icy snow, something rare in their parts. It had started to fall harder and the sky had gone dark early.

Before she knew it, it was five o'clock. She stretched and started gathering her things. And wondered where Trent was. She wanted to tell him what she found in person.

And, well, she wanted to see him, too.

After putting their lunch dishes in the dishwasher, she leaned over and picked up Amanda. After changing her diaper, she decided to walk around a bit. Trent had told her to make herself at home.

She really was eager to see a bit more of the house besides his study, the bathroom and the kitchen. "Amanda, where do you think this door leads to?" she murmured as she walked to the back of the room.

Peeking on the other side, she couldn't help but gasp. It was the biggest darn dining room she'd ever seen in her life. At least twenty people could sit at the table.

Unable to stop herself, she stepped across the hardwood floors and onto the thickest, fanciest, reddest Oriental carpet she'd ever seen in her life. Next thing she knew, she was running her fingers along the dark wood of the mahogany table.

One touch led to another. She patted the soft fabric of one of the chairs. A luxurious tapestry, woven in shades of ivory and white, covered the seat of each one. "I'd be half-afraid to sit in one of these," she said. "It would be just my luck if I spilled spaghetti sauce right on it."

Worried she was going to ruin the fabric by standing too close to it, she walked to the far wall, where a pair of china cabinets stood. Each held a wide array of porcelain, sterling silver and crystal.

And for some reason, they were what held her attention more than anything—because those were items a person didn't buy because they were needed. They weren't used or collected by people like her. Or even by people like the Riddells used to be.

The set of six Waterford goblets were for society folks. Rich people. Fancy people.

It all made her kind of sad. It was as if with that one collection of silver salt shakers the gap between them got bigger and bigger, leaving a chasm so wide and deep there was almost no way she could ever jump across it. How had the two of them gotten so far apart? Since when had fancy things been a part of Trent's life?

And since when had she even cared?

In her arms, Amanda fussed. Jolene patted her back. "It's okay, baby. We'll get on out of here in just a minute."

"I hope not," Trent said from the doorway.

Her heart beating like crazy, she turned to face him. "What's wrong?"

As he looked at Jolene, Trent fought to keep his emotions in check. For an instant, he was sure everything he was feeling was written all over his face—tenderness for a baby he didn't even know, longing for a woman he'd kept at an emotional distance, and frustration at the weather outside.

But none of those things were what he wanted her to see. What mattered was her security. "It's snowing outside. Real hard."

Her wary expression cleared. "Is that all? I can handle driving in snow, Trent."

"Have you looked out the window? It's not just snowing hard, it's a near whiteout. That, combined with how dark it is out, means it would be pretty darn treacherous for you to be out in it."

She held Amanda a little tighter. "Trent, I need to get on home."

"Stay here."

"That's just not possible. I've got to work tomorrow."

"You won't if this keeps up. Look, I've got a half dozen empty bedrooms. Pick one. Tomorrow when the weather clears, you can be on your way."

But instead of seeing just how reasonable his idea was, instead of thanking him for the offer, Jolene only looked cornered. "I can't do that."

Over by the door was Amanda's carrier. Making a split decision, he retrieved it, then gently took the baby from her.

He needed to speak to Jolene without anything between them. He needed to make her see the truth of things.

Miraculously, little Amanda settled into her carrier with hardly more than a sigh and a squirm. When he was sure she was settled, Trent stepped toward Jolene, eager to close the space between them. "Why not?"

"You know why."

He needed her to see that his intentions were completely honorable. That he was safe. That being here with him was the right thing to do. "What are you worried about? Are you worried about people talking?"

"I think it's a little late for me to be thinking like that, don't you?" she asked. "I mean, people are already

making up stories about me being worse than I am—
and I thought that was hard to top." Her voice thick
with bitterness, she shook her head. "Sometimes I just
wish everyone would mind their own business instead
of mine."

"I've wished that a time or two myself."

"The thing is, I know I should be used to it. Even
when I was little I never seemed to be good enough."

Unable to help himself, he grabbed her hand and
tugged her to a dining room chair and sat her down.
She perched on the edge, as though she was afraid to
break it.

He pulled another chair out and sat across from her.
"There's not a thing wrong with you, Jo. In fact, you're
just about everything that's ever been right." Searching
her gaze, he continued. "Do you know what finally
made me see the light and think about you differently?"

Instead of a sassy remark, she merely shook her head.

"It was Bob."

"Bob? What do you mean?"

"He was the one who was singing your praises like
nobody's business. And I'll tell you what, he was right.
People like you, Jolene. And let me tell you something
else. There's more than a few people in this town who
admire you."

"For what? Working in a bar and getting knocked up?"

"For making the best of tough situations."

He wanted to gather her in his arms, but every instinct in his being told him that wasn't what she needed.
So, he did something even harder. He brought up the
past. "Don't you think I know what happened to you
at your house, Jolene?" he whispered. When pure pain
filtered through her eyes, he scooted even closer, so

their knees were touching, and only a haze of unspoken thoughts lay between them.

Pressing on, he said, "I remember you showing up with bruises on your face. I remember you coming over and being hungry."

"Don't go there, Trent," she commanded, her voice hard.

"Why?" he asked softly. "Your daddy made you what you are. What he did, and what your mother didn't do— it broke my heart. It still does," he admitted.

Slowly, she met his gaze. Then, too quickly, she averted her eyes again. "It was a long time ago."

"I know. But it doesn't mean I don't remember."

After a pause, she said, "I remember it well." Her cheeks colored as she added, "And how y'all let me come over, at all hours of the day or night."

He hadn't forgotten any of that, either.

"Those days, living next to y'all, they were some of my best," she admitted.

"I know."

Her chin popped up. "Trent?"

"I know your daddy got drunk and forgot to buy milk and slapped you when you got in the way. And I know he took off when you were fourteen and you and your momma took care of things the best you could. And it wasn't too good at all." He feared other things had happened, too. But they weren't anything he was ever going to bring up.

Her green eyes looked almost luminescent. "Out in Big Spring… How did you know about that?"

"Because I wanted to. We might have drifted apart, but I still asked about you. And every once in a while I'd hear some news. What I heard broke my heart, Jo.

Only when I started doing the circuit did I lose track of you." He paused, then made himself continue. "Along the way, I think I lost sight of what was important. Family…and people I care about."

For one split second, her whole expression opened and pure pain burned brightly. Uncovered and bare— there for him to see.

Making his whole body ache with dismay. Trent reached out, traced two fingers along her arm and encouraged her without words to be honest with him.

Her mouth opened. He held his breath. Then she closed her lips abruptly and stood up. "I—I can't do this. I can't talk about the past. Not even with you."

Not even with you. And that, Trent realized, was what all of this was really about.

They were closer than most people realized. Closer than they realized. And just as she turned on her heel, just when she was about to run away from him, Trent got to his feet and wrapped his arms around Jolene.

And when she tried to break away, he skimmed his palm along her cheek, gentling her.

And then he kissed her.

At first, she stood motionless. Stunned.

That was okay, he didn't mind. He knew how to kiss, and he knew how to encourage her. Tenderly, he nipped at her bottom lip. Sucked gently. Traced the line of her lips with his tongue.

Then, finally, with a sigh, she relaxed and kissed him back.

He held her closer, wrapped his arms around her and gently rubbed her back. Enjoyed the feel of her body, so lean and slim, against his chest and hips. The kiss deepened. His heartbeat clicked into double time. But the rest of him felt as though he was going into slow motion, analyzing all the changes in her body.

Her breasts were softer. Her hips slightly wider. But there also seemed to be a new tenderness between them that hadn't existed before. That hadn't even been there when they'd had sex on the floor of her apartment.

But maybe that had just been the whiskey's doing?

Tilting his head, he lightened his touch, kissed her sweetly, ran a hand farther down her back to cup her rear and press against her, just so she'd know that he wanted her.

But that was all it took for her to stiffen and pull away. "Trent? Is *this* what you've been telling me I don't have to worry about?"

He would have snapped a retort, but he knew Jolene better than that. She was flustered because she was feeling the same thing he was—desire.

"I'm sorry. I know I shouldn't have kissed you. But I know that kiss meant something…and I know the feelings I had were mutual, too."

"Oh, I know. But that doesn't mean it's okay."

He stepped back. "Please stay. I promise, I won't touch you. Please, if you go, I'm going to have to follow, to make sure you get home safely. And to be honest, it's miserable out there. I'd much rather stay here in front of the fire."

"I'm not going to sleep with you tonight."

"I don't want you to," he replied.

She studied his face, searched for lies. But when she found none, she nodded. "Okay then, I'll stay."

"I'm glad." After a moment, he picked up the baby's carrier and led Jolene into the living room. It was time to get them settled, and to figure out dinner…and to wrap his mind around the fact that they were two big, fat liars.

Chapter Seventeen

Had she ever really trusted anyone? As Jolene chopped up vegetables for a stir-fry, she tried to remember.

Maybe she'd trusted her mother. Well, she'd trusted her love. But she hadn't trusted her ability to do the best for them. Her mother had been worn down too much by life and the disappointments that came with it to take the hard path. For Carrie Arnold, anything easy had been the only choice that made sense.

On one level, Jolene understood that completely.

But now that she was a mom herself, Jolene just wasn't sure if simply loving your child was enough. Sometimes the hard road was the one to take, even if it caused pain.

"Jo, you doing okay over there?" Trent asked from the other side of the kitchen.

Her knife paused on the wooden chopping board. "I'm fine. Why?"

"No reason," he said as he finished expertly slicing the steak into perfect bite-size strips. "Except that you look like you're about to beat up on that poor red pepper something awful."

"I guess I have," she said in surprise. Just to get

his gander, she quipped, "I must have been thinking about you."

He grunted. "Ouch."

Jolene smiled back. This was how he'd been all evening, gently joking, carefully keeping her spirits high and her nerves at bay.

Completely opposite of the way he'd been when he'd reminded her of the past. And there had been nothing teasing at all when they'd kissed. Then, he'd been a hundred percent all male and in command. Her knees would have gone weak, and she would have swooned... if she'd ever been that kind of girl.

"I'm surprised a bachelor like you knows how to cook. I would have thought you'd be making due with cold cuts."

"I started eating healthy years ago. You can't hold on to the back of a bull with just frozen pizzas and sandwiches in your stomach."

Imagining his life on the road, placing his will against a riled up bull in the ring, never failed to make her heart contract. "I suppose you can't," she acknowledged. "It's funny, but when you were on the circuit, I looked for your name all the time. But now that you've been back, it's easy for me to forget that you're 'Trent Riddell, World Champion Bull Rider.'"

He laughed. "Don't you know you're supposed to whisper those words in reverence?" Holding up his arm, he said, "Don't forget, I took a lot of knocks to get that title."

Instantly, she sobered. "I hate that thought."

"I'm just kidding around. You know I'm fine."

"Now you are. I've heard stories, Trent. You've been badly hurt. Especially this last time."

"I'm healing." He shook his arm slightly and frowned. "Well, I almost am. Now that the cast is off and I've started rehab, I'll be better than ever." He picked up a chunk of lettuce and started carefully tearing off the leaves one-handed. "I've been on my own a long time now. Cooking's a good thing. And as far as being a champion and all, well, that only gets you as far as a couple of fan clubs. All that really matters is what I do the next time I'm on a bull."

Now that she'd finished her portion of the chopping, she carried her bowl of vegetables over to him and watched him finish. "Trent, don't be silly. We both know there's a lot more to you than just your ability to hold on for eight seconds."

"Maybe. Maybe not. I've come to learn it's the only part that anyone really cares about."

"You think?"

"I know."

"Maybe the problem is that you're hanging out around the wrong people." Realizing how that sounded, she held up a hand. "Present company excluded."

Looking her over, he grinned. "Is that right?"

There was that tension again, filtering upward, pulling her into its web. Making the atmosphere between them turn on its side and heat up.

She felt his gaze graze her lips. In response, she licked her bottom lip. And then felt that traitorous tingle again. All of a sudden, she couldn't help but think about how his hands had felt on her bare skin. Strong, but so gentle. Assured. She remembered just how perfect his body had felt against her own. Trent was all tan, smooth skin and layers upon layers of muscle.

For just a little while, he'd been all hers…and for

just a few moments, she'd been completely taken care of. Cuddled. Loved.

Of course, that had been a silly fantasy—something certainly not grounded in reality. But sometimes, well, she wished it had been real.

Oh, but she wished she was stronger where he was concerned!

"Jo, how about a beer? Or a glass of wine?"

Hmm. Maybe she wasn't the only one who was feeling their attraction. "I'd love a glass of wine."

"White or red?"

"Whatever's handy."

"How about we share a bottle of red?"

"I'll get the glasses."

After he'd poured them both a glass, he heated up the wok and started sautéing.

"Why don't you turn on some Christmas music in the other room? Amanda might like that."

"Sure."

And so Trent cooked and she danced to "Rockin' Around the Christmas Tree," holding Amanda in her arms as she twirled.

Amanda cooed and squealed. And Jolene started to think that maybe this was one of the most perfect nights of her life.

Their simple dinner was good. She helped him wash the dishes. Afterward, she put Amanda to sleep, and then she stood by his side as they looked out the windows at the snow.

Maybe it was the wine. Or maybe it was the easy companionship they'd somehow managed to find again after a very long absence. But now Jolene felt that they were back on even ground. They were close again. They'd become friends.

"Hey, Jo?" he asked after a while.

"Uh-huh?"

"What should we do about Amanda?"

Warily, she glanced at his profile. Trent was still staring ahead. His posture as easy as always. But there was an edge to his jaw. A tenseness that made her think that maybe his question had been stewing for some time.

"Guess it depends on you."

Slowly he looked her way. "What are you saying?"

"It's easy enough to understand. If you want to be involved and see her lots, that's good. If you don't, I'll deal with that, too."

He moved a little closer, invading her space. "So don't you think you deserve better than that?"

Jolene knew she did. But she'd given up on fairy-tale endings. But did she tell the man who'd impregnated her but never returned her calls that, yes, she did think she deserved better than what he was offering?

"Don't worry about me," she said.

Reaching out, he gripped the wooden pane in front of him. His knuckles turned white. "You really do think I'm the father, don't you?"

He might as well have slapped her. "We're back to that, huh?"

"I'm just saying…we haven't gotten the results back yet…"

"You might be waiting for that phone call with bated breath, but I'm not. I know what we did, and I know how I got pregnant." So tired of defending her past to him, she said, "I know my reputation. But I haven't slept with as many men as you seem to think I have. I know who the father is. And I did try to contact him."

This time she was the one turning away. This time she was the one who bit back what she really wanted to say. "I think I'm going to go to my room, if you don't mind."

He looked at his watch. "It's only nine o'clock. Are you sure? We could watch a movie or something." He flashed a smile. "Maybe *White Christmas* is on."

That was exactly what she did not need to be doing with him. Just imagining sitting next to him on the couch, watching sappy Christmas movies about finding true love, would most certainly set her off into the deep end. "Maybe another time. I'm pretty tired. It's been a full day, you know. And I'm kind of anxious to take a bath."

"I can understand that. Hey, you want one of my T-shirts or something to sleep in?"

"That would be perfect. Thanks."

"I'll be right back."

He darted off and she pretended she wasn't going to really enjoy wearing something of his.

Two minutes later, he handed her a well-worn soft undershirt. "There's extra toothbrushes and stuff in the guest bathroom."

"I'll be fine."

"My room's upstairs. I'll keep the door open in case you need anything…"

"I won't."

"I know. But maybe Amanda might?"

Jolene steeled her mind to ignore that hint of question in his tone. Honestly, if she didn't know better, she would think Trent was actually looking for a reason to hold Amanda.

Though it was tempting to immediately accept his offer, she forced herself to remember all the times she'd called him and he didn't answer. To remember that he was still awaiting test results. Most likely, he'd even played her messages. But he'd made the conscious decision to ignore them.

However, there was nothing to be gained by revisiting all that again.

She lifted her chin slightly. "If Amanda needs anything at all, I'll take care of her. It's what I do."

A flicker of pain—and maybe, irritation?—passed over his face. "I see."

"We'll try not to wake you."

"I wouldn't mind if you did."

But she would.

"I'll see you in the morning," she said quickly, then walked away before she could rethink things. Walked away before she got weak and ruined everything by kissing him. Again.

Or worse…started falling in love with him. All over again.

Chapter Eighteen

He'd been overdoing it. His body was still healing from getting stomped on by Diablo, and he hadn't been taking enough care with his arm.

Sick to death of not moving at a hundred percent, Trent grimaced as he pushed away the pain.

Yeah. It was a physical thing. That was why he was up at three in the morning. That was why he was hobbling around the downstairs, trying not to disturb Amanda or Jolene.

That was why he'd tossed and turned all night and had hardly slept more than a half hour at a time. His arm was sore. So was his back. His neck didn't feel too good.

Yeah, it was only his body—not his mind—that was in turmoil.

Yeah, right.

Trent grimaced. No matter how much he wanted to kid himself, even he couldn't pretend he was up and restless because of a few injuries. He knew why he was up and about. The fact of the matter was that he couldn't get Jolene Arnold off his mind.

Yep, she'd settled into his psyche and wasn't going to leave for nothing.

But even now as he popped two ibuprofen and gulped down some water from the tap, Trent found his mind drifting back to their conversation. And to the way she'd looked more than a little wary when he'd suggested they watch a movie.

What had bothered her? Had her refusal been all about him being a jerk about the test results? Or was she worried about being alone with him?

Thinking of their recent kiss, he groaned. He sure hadn't minded kissing her. In fact, he'd been more than eager to do it. He always had. Kissing Jolene was pretty incredible. She never failed to smell faintly of lemons, and she fit just right in his arms.

Her figure was amazing, but that wasn't why he liked holding her. No, he liked holding her because she was Jolene.

After searching through the cabinets, he found a microwavable heating pad. After zapping it for a few moments, he sprawled out on the couch in the living room and set the pad on his shoulder. The heat brought immediate relief. Gingerly, he moved his arm back and forth, working the muscle, setting it in motion. Little by little, the cramp eased, bringing him relief.

If only he could find something to ease his mind that easily.

What was it about Jolene that had him all twisted in knots? Was it because of Amanda...or was it something else?

She was pretty, smart and liked to laugh. But more than any of that, she was different.

The thought stilled him.

Fact was, Jolene was as much a part of his childhood as his older brothers' pounding or his mother's laughter.

She'd been a constant and he'd liked her very much, indeed. When he saw the fingerprint bruises on her arm, he'd been shocked. His dad had been gruff and obstinate. He'd never been afraid to swat his butt if it had been warranted, but he'd never grabbed any of his children in anger.

And his father would have stepped in front of a charging bull instead of marking their mother. Any of them would have.

And Trent knew their feelings were tenfold that about Ginny.

But Jo had just shrugged off her hurts with a watery laugh. Just like she'd refused to talk about her split lip. Or the welt on her thigh.

And then they'd moved on up. Eventually, she'd moved away, too. And when he'd heard, he'd been tempted to ask his dad to cart her back. Because even at eight years of age, Trent had known that Jolene Arnold's life had just gone from bad to worse.

And here, all this time later, it had become easier to forget about that. Until tonight, he'd pushed her pain and his guilt to the back of his mind because it hurt too bad.

Now what did that say about him, really?

That he was as selfish and self-centered as he suspected?

As he was stewing on that, he heard a peep coming from Jo's room.

Getting to his feet, he crossed the living room, and walked down the hall to her room, stood there and listened.

And heard that little peep again. Amanda Rose was fussing.

As quietly as he could, Trent turned her doorknob and looked inside.

At the foot of the queen-size bed was the Pack 'N Play. And there, squirming on her back like a doodle bug, was Amanda. Bright blue eyes fastened on his, studying him. Then she smiled in recognition.

His heart melted.

Unable to help himself, he stepped in and glanced Jolene's way.

Jo was sprawled out on her stomach, not a stitch of covers on top of her. She'd tossed the pillow away, so she was flat on the bed, her blond hair all this way and that, half covering her profile, the rest flowing across her shoulders and back. His T-shirt had ridden up to her waist, and a tiny pair of pink bikini panties covered only a small portion of that very fine rear end.

She was as pretty as a picture. Better than that, actually. She looked like every man's secret desire. She looked like Jolene.

Amanda peeped again.

"Hey, honey," he whispered as he bent down. "Whatcha doin' up this time of night?"

At the sound of his voice, she turned her head to him and blinked. Her perfect cupid bow lips opened. Her body was in a one piece snap-up pajama suit. It was white and was covered with drawings of a little brown dog running around. Her feet kicked and wiggled.

Right then and there, Trent fell in love.

When her mouth opened again, and a fierce, irritated look appeared on her face, Trent chuckled. "Come on, sweetheart. I know what you want," he drawled as he bent down and scooped her up in his arms.

After one last look at Jolene, Trent carried Amanda to the kitchen.

Years ago, he'd fed Ginny bottles. And all day long, he'd watched Jolene feed them to Amanda. He knew what to do.

And bless Jo's organized heart, she had a bottle all ready to go, its liner filled with powdered formula. All it needed was some warm water. Quickly, he poured a bit of water into a measuring cup and set it to heating up in the microwave.

Less than two minutes later, he was sitting on the couch, a dishcloth over one shoulder, and giving Miss Amanda a snack. She sucked greedily, holding one of his fingers tightly, as if she was afraid he was going to leave her.

"I'm not going anywhere, sugar," he murmured. "I'm all yours."

She blinked. Reminding him of Ginny's, Amanda's eyes were the exact same shade of blue. The color of bluebonnets in early May, before the heat came and made everything fade.

Jolene's door opened. "Amanda?" she called out, her voice in a panic. "Amanda?"

"I've got her, Jo," he answered, doing his best to not startle the baby.

Obviously half-asleep, Jolene padded toward him, still dressed only in his T-shirt. "What's going on? Why do you have her?"

"She was fussing."

"I'm sorry. Did she wake you? I didn't even hear her." Quickly closing in the space, Jo looked ready to take her baby and run.

"Don't fret. I was up anyway. She just made a little peep so I went to check on her."

"I can't believe I didn't hear her. I bet you're more than ready to—"

"Are you kidding? We've been having a good ol' time, drinking milk and catching up. Why don't you go on back to bed? I'll put her back in a little while."

"I couldn't." But she yawned as she said it, making Trent recall Bob's words. About how Jolene had been all alone—pretty much all her life—doing everything herself. Even working until the middle of the night...

"Come over here and sit with us, then," he said. Motioning to the down throw that was resting on the armrest, he murmured, "If you're cold, you can use that to cover up."

She stiffened as she noticed her bare legs. "Shoot. I didn't meant to come out here half-naked."

"I didn't mind." Not a bit.

She tugged down the shirt and frowned.

He couldn't resist teasing her. "I've seen you in less. You're not shocking me, I promise. Shoot, I only have on bottoms. We're fine."

Without another word, she took his advice and pulled the blanket over her. Tucked her legs under herself. Yawned again.

"She's just about done."

Trent looked at Amanda and realized Jo was right. The baby's eyelids were at half-mast and the formula was almost gone. Expertly, he popped her to his shoulder and coaxed a burp.

Jolene smiled. "I never would have guessed you would be so good with her."

"I'm a man of many talents, Jo," he drawled. "Don't you forget that."

"I'll try not to."

Within the past few minutes, Amanda had fallen asleep in his arms. Her head was tucked into the curve of his elbow, the rest of her was cuddled close. Heating him up.

Feeling a little stiff, he stretched out his leg. When the baby fussed, he carefully rearranged her, so she was soon comfortably tucked in snug beside him. He sighed with pleasure.

Holding the baby felt right. It brought back fond memories of holding Ginny, and something more intense and satisfying, too.

Closing his eyes, he breathed Amanda's scent and felt himself relax even more.

"I…I should take her back to bed," Jolene murmured, her voice strained.

His eyes popped open. "Is there a need? She seems happy as a clam to me." Patting the couch, he smiled at Jo. "Why don't you just sit with me for a bit?"

"Why?" She looked at him. In that stare was a whole lot that wasn't said. Yet again they had that same connection they couldn't ignore. Once more, he was hyper-aware of each movement of her body. Of the way her slim arms folded the blanket against her chest. Of the way she sleepily brushed back the wayward curls off her neck. Making him itch to traipse his fingers there, too.

But of course he couldn't say any of that. "Because I like your company. Because sitting next to you feels good," he said simply, giving Jolene the only answer he could. The only answer that he was comfortable with, anyway.

"It does," she murmured with some surprise. "Almost like old times. But better."

He knew what she meant. Fact was, sitting there, in the middle of the night, with snow outside his windows and a sleepy baby curled next to his belly—well that was pretty much the nicest thing that had happened to him in quite some time.

However, the new awareness that had become a constant between them was nothing like they'd known.

"Why don't you stretch out some?" he asked, keeping his voice slow and steady.

As if that was the only bit of encouragement she'd been waiting for, Jolene stretched out her legs and shifted to her side.

Unable to help himself, he reached out and rearranged the blanket, slipping it over her arms a little more snugly. And then he gave in to temptation and brushed back the hair from her face.

She smiled softly.

Time passed. Maybe it was five minutes. Maybe it was more like twenty. Around them, the house settled and snow fluttered against the windowpanes—flakes illuminated as they caught the light from one of the outside lights running along the walkway.

Beside him, Amanda squeaked and shifted, teasing a smile from him. Jolene's eyelids slid shut. Her breathing slowed, turning all deep and even.

"'Night, Jo," he whispered. Then, he reached out and brushed his knuckles along the smooth planes of her cheek, fingered the silky strands of her tresses and realized that her skin was still soft. And that she still smelled faintly of lemons.

Just like she had all those years ago. When he'd hugged her goodbye and had bussed a sloppy wet kiss to her cheek.

Back when they'd drifted apart and she'd somehow become just a girl he'd used to know.

Chapter Nineteen

Jo woke up in a haze of warm blanket, suede leather and velvet pillow. Her mouth felt like cotton, making her realize that she'd slept with her mouth open again.

She swallowed hard and took a minute to figure out where she was. Her whole body was stiff, signaling that she was in unfamiliar territory. Little by little, reality set in. Riddell Ranch. Snow. Amanda up at night. Couch. Trent.

And then she caught the inevitable—the unmistakable scent of Trent, lying there, right next to her. She sneaked a peek. He was sound asleep, sleeping as quietly as their baby. Looking peaceful and almost boyish. Looking as gorgeous as ever.

Oh, Lord have mercy!

Unable to not take advantage of the moment, and not even sure that she wanted to, Jolene let her gaze rest on him. He was sprawled out, and she couldn't help but smile as she looked at his bare shoulders, at the scars that littered his tan, smooth chest.

The muscles that marked his biceps. And his pectorals. The line of faint blond hair that snaked down the center of his belly and disappeared into the unbuttoned waistband of his faded Levi's.

Trent Riddell was gorgeous, it was true. His cheeks were covered in stubble, his blond hair sticking up near his forehead. And he was snoring.

In between them, snug as a bug, was Amanda Rose. Their baby.

And for the briefest of moments, Jolene let herself pretend that this was their life. That they really were a family. But then, just as quickly, she pushed that dream away. Even when Trent finally did accept the truth about Amanda, he wasn't going to turn into Prince Charming and make all her worries disappear.

For that matter, she'd still be pretty darn far from Cinderella, too.

No, the most she could hope for was a congenial future, one in which they took each other's phone calls, Trent would pay child support, and most likely help pay for Amanda's clothes and doctor bills, too. Maybe every now and then they'd spend a day together once a month. When he was in town.

She needed to get up and give herself a reality check. It was time to go home to her apartment, check in with Cheryl about sitting, and head on over to work.

There, she'd have no problem remembering that they each had their place in Electra. And though those paths might cross every once in a while, their places were never going to mesh.

Not for long, anyway.

As carefully as possible, she scooted off the couch and ran to the bathroom. Less than ten minutes later, she was back in her clothes and was gathering Amanda's things in the kitchen.

And ten minutes after that, she was in the covered carport, turning on her car.

As she headed back inside, she found Trent watching her from the doorway, scowling.

"Jolene, what the heck are you doing?"

"Getting ready to be on my way."

"Do you need your vision checked? Ice and snow have frozen just about everything solid. The roads are going to be like an ice rink."

"It's not snowing now. And the weather's better. I'm sure the roads will be fine." If she was lucky.

Clad only in his jeans, which were still unbuttoned at the waist, Trent marched out to her car, reached inside and pulled out the key. "You are not driving anywhere."

"Trent, you're not my daddy."

He looped his fingers around her wrist and tugged her into the house. "And thank goodness I'm not," he blurted. "I can't think of a worse person to be."

Though she privately agreed, she still didn't appreciate being manhandled. "Trent, stop."

"Why? Why on earth do you need to leave right this minute?"

"Because it's time."

"You better be more specific, sugar."

"All right. It's Thursday, and I'm working tonight." His eyes narrowed. "And?"

"And I need to put on fresh clothes. I need to bathe Amanda and get more formula and diapers." She needed to get away from temptation and dreams.

"Fine. I'll drive you."

"There's no need."

"There's *every* need. No way am I going to let you on the road by yourself. What if something happened to you?" His voice rose. "What if something happened to Amanda? What would we do then?"

We? Her heart beat a little faster. She couldn't find fault with his reasoning. But it didn't mean she had to give in gracefully. "Chances are we'd be fine."

He rolled his eyes. "Well, then, shoot. Let's go ahead and gamble with her life, why don't we?"

She sputtered as they walked into the kitchen. "All right. Thank you for taking us home."

"You're welcome. Now, let's make some coffee, then we'll get ready to go." He directed a firm glare her way. "And don't you start fussing and complaining about that, either. You know I can't do a thing without coffee."

"I'll make it, you go get dressed."

With a pause, he looked at himself, as if he suddenly realized he was only wearing a pair of worn, unbuttoned jeans.

"Sounds good," he muttered. "Make the coffee strong, would you? I have a feeling it's going to be a long day."

TAKING THE STAIRS AS QUICKLY as he could, Trent called himself a fool. When he'd gone to sleep last night, he'd really thought something had changed between them. That they'd become something other than old friends. Or uneasy former lovers. Or, shoot…parents.

But obviously Jolene hadn't been feeling the same way.

He walked straight through his bedroom to his bathroom. After brushing his teeth and splashing water on his face, he took stock. The man staring back at him in the mirror looked about like he always did. A little on the thin side—probably a good eight pounds lighter than his usual weight. And his hair was kind of scraggly, too. He'd been so fixated on his body healing that he'd forgotten most everything else to do with his upkeep. He needed a shave, but that was nothing new.

No, the only thing new about him were all the scars. Riding bulls wasn't an easy thing, not even on a good day. A lot of times, the bull came out the winner, and his ribs lived to tell the tale.

Turning around, he inspected his back and winced. Yes, some were worse than others.

As he looked at the puckered circle on his right tricep, he frowned. That had been from a drunken night and a barbed wire fence. He should've had it doctored.

But he'd never seen the need. Now, though, the scars seemed to serve as an illustration about how much damage he'd done to his life without hardly a second glance behind him.

He was still thinking about the wreck of his body after pulling on his boots and throwing on a T-shirt and a flannel button-down.

In the kitchen, Jolene was holding Amanda in her carrier. Two plastic coffee cups were on the counter. "I thought I'd put them in to-go cups so we wouldn't have to wait."

"That's fine," he said as he shrugged into his coat. "I mean, that's fine, if you're in such an all-fired hurry and all."

"It's not that. It's just time for me to go home."

"Of course." Well, there was no reason to delay the inevitable. "Let's get going, then." He led the way out to his Ford and helped Jolene secure Amanda's car seat.

He switched into four-wheel drive and then edged out of the carport. Almost immediately, the tires squeaked a bit as they attempted to grab a hold on the icy surface.

Trent was no wimp. Over the years, he'd driven just about all types of vehicle, in just about any type of weather. But this was different. This time he was carrying Amanda. And Jolene.

And this time he really wished they were making breakfast together instead of trucking out to the highway.

He glanced her way as they crunched down the long driveway. "Seat belt on tight?"

"Of course."

"Good."

Once they'd cleared the gate, he pulled out and turned left. When the back of the truck fishtailed, he gritted his teeth and tried not to swear.

Next to him, Jolene tensed up. "I guess making you take me home was pretty foolish. The roads are awful."

"They are bad," he agreed. "But there's nothing wrong with wanting to get to your job, or to care for your daughter. If you need her home, then that's what is important."

"I do need her home," she murmured.

Trent could think of nothing else to say to that. So he concentrated on driving slow and steady. Luckily there weren't a lot of turns in the road in between his home and hers. He was thankful for that. The less braking on ice he had to do, the better.

"But the truth is, being with you was making me nervous," she added.

The truck squealed and slid as he slammed on the brakes.

"Trent!"

Damn. "I'm sorry." Putting both hands on the wheel, he steadied the vehicle. And while he was at it, he tried to steady his pulse, too.

Once things were going well again, he glanced her way. "Care to tell me what you meant by that?"

"About being nervous?"

"Uh-huh."

"I think what I said was pretty clear." She looked at him sideways. "I mean, don't you think?"

"No. Did I do something to upset you?"

"That's not what I meant," she said quickly. "Trent, I wasn't talking about anything you've done. It's all me. I get nervous around you."

"And why is that?"

"If I tell you, do you promise not to freak out and get us in a car wreck?"

"I'll do my best."

"That's not good enough."

"I promise, Jolene. What do I do? I really need to know."

"Sometimes—not all the time, mind you..."

"Yes?"

"Well. Sometimes...I just start thinking about things."

They were almost at her apartment. And once they got there, like a psychic, he knew exactly what was going to happen. She was going to tear out of the car like nobody's business, and he was going to be left with a hell of a lot of questions.

And nothing but time and a wide expanse of icy road to contemplate them. "Please. Tell me. What do you think about?"

"About us."

"What about us?" He almost yelled it, he was gettin' so damn irritated. Because, sure enough, there they were. Pulling into her complex.

"Maybe we should talk about this another day..."

He pulled into a parking place and almost pushed the automatic locks down so she couldn't escape.

"Jo. Spit it out. I won't get mad."

She put her hand on the door. "All right. Here it is. Sometimes, when we're in each other's company, and things are going fine…I start imagining the two of us together, and I know I shouldn't."

"Together? Like on your floor?"

"No, Trent," she said with what sounded like extreme patience. "I mean together, like a fairy tale. Like a couple. Like a relationship."

She said the word *relationship* as if she'd been getting tutored by Dr. Phil.

He could almost feel his face turning as white as the snow.

His silence seemed to set her off. "Oh, for Pete's sake, Trent. Sometimes, I swear you make me crazy. *C-R-A-Z-Y.*"

And while he was sitting there, scared stiff, she clambered out of her seat, hopped out of the truck, turned around, grabbed Amanda in record time and slammed both doors.

Like the biggest jerk imaginable, he watched her trudge toward her door, fish out a giant silver ring from the depths of her monstrous purse and, finally, unlock that door.

He watched her carry her daughter inside and shut the door behind her.

And he sat there staring at the door, wishing she wasn't now gone from his sight.

And still he sat there, truck running, heart racing, head pounding…because sometimes, he knew he also sort of felt the very same way.

Chapter Twenty

Yes, the roads were in bad shape. Yes, he had better things to do than hang out at Bob's, but sometimes what a man did and what a man ought to do didn't necessarily coincide.

Which was all the justification Trent needed to turn left out of Jolene's apartment complex instead of right, and carefully traverse the lone mile to Bronco Bob's.

It had just hit noon. Jolene said she wasn't going in until three or four.

And though most folks weren't there for the beer, more than a couple had braved the elements for a burger and congenial company.

Trent pulled up a stool in the shadows next to the wall, ordered himself a bacon cheddar burger and an ice-cold Coke.

While he was waiting, he visited with Carter, who was cleaning glasses, and listened to the news of the day—which, of course, was the current crappy weather conditions.

And then—speak of the devil—Addison Thomas waltzed in.

Trent was glad he was sitting at the far corner of the bar, because the guy didn't notice him right away. That suited him just fine. He wanted to see what that guy was like before he went and told him to leave Jolene alone.

When Addison took a seat at the other end of the bar, he started joking with Carter.

That was fine.

But then Addison started asking questions about a certain blonde.

That was not.

"So…you're good friends with Jolene, aren't you, Carter?"

Carter set down the wineglass he'd been holding. "Good enough."

"Is she seeing anyone, do you know?"

Carter darted a look Trent's way before he answered Addison. "I really couldn't say."

That, of course, made Trent swallow hard. He wasn't seeing Jolene…

"Well, I have to tell you, I wish I could figure her out."

"What seems to be confusing you?"

"I don't understand why she seems so intent on being alone. She's a real nice gal, and that baby of hers is a sweetie, too. She needs a man in her life."

"A man, huh?" Carter looked as though he was fighting a smile as he picked up another glass. "I wouldn't go telling her that."

"I haven't. Shoot, that's why I'm sitting here, talking with you." Addison looked mildly embarrassed as he swallowed back the last of his beer before signaling for another one. "It's just I wish she'd give me a chance. I mean, I know I've got to be a heck of a lot better than that bastard who gave her a baby and then took off."

Down in the shadows, Trent choked. Carter glanced

his way, then looked down at the glass in his hand again. "I wouldn't be talking about Jolene like that."

"Why not? I'm not faulting her. I mean, she's got a child to support. It's not her fault that her mystery man never stepped up. I feel sorry for her, that's all."

Trent's collar was starting to feel too tight, which served him right, because what the hell was he doing, hanging out in a bar in the middle of the day anyway?

However, overriding all that uncomfortableness was the sense that Addison was right. Jolene was a sweet woman. And it was a shame she was doing everything on her own…and everyone knew it, too.

From the other side of the bar, Bob cleared his throat. "Jolene's a friend of mine, Addison. I think you've gossiped about her enough."

Addison held up two hands. "I don't mean no disrespect—"

But here he was, about to go on another Jolene tangent, Trent thought drily.

When Carter looked as if he was about to rub the glass he was drying raw, Trent knew it was time to get involved. Shoot, probably *way* past time. Stepping into the other man's line of vision. Addison started for a moment. "Trent. Hey. I didn't see you there."

"I didn't think you did," he replied, keeping his voice slow and easy. "Listen, I appreciate you worrying over Jolene, but I just wanted you to know that there's no need."

"Why not?"

To Trent's dismay, both Carter and Bob leaned in closer, just to get a good earful.

Well, guess there was no turning back. "Well, Jo and I have been seeing each other lately."

"Really? I thought y'all were just old acquaintances."

There was something about that *acquaintance* word that chafed Trent something awful. Maybe it was the insinuation that there really had been something in their past. Or maybe it was the veiled hint that there certainly couldn't be anything between the two of them now.

But whatever it was, it got him talking. "We're more than that."

On the other side of the bar, Carter hastily put up a hand to cover a cough.

Maybe it was because of the way they'd woken up together, snuggled on the couch, peaceful, with a baby in between them. Or maybe it was because he was tired of Jolene Arnold getting screwed around by men in her life, himself included.

Or that Addison was starting to seem just about the biggest jerk he'd ever met...

But whatever the reason, Trent saw red. Going on the offensive, he slipped off his bar stool and approached the idiot. "Addison, I'm going to give you some advice," he said softly. "And it would be real good of you to listen to it, 'cause I'm not in the habit of repeating myself. I don't know how your family works, but the men in my family do not ever discuss the women in their lives in bars. Or with cocky little bastards."

But instead of being cowed—which would have been so much smarter—Addison raised his brows. "So what are you saying Jolene is to you? A woman in your life?"

Time seemed to stand still as he processed those words. And realized it was time to move forward or start doing the backtracking two-step.

"She's much more than that. She's my fiancée," he blurted because he wasn't the type of man to back down.

It was why he was extremely successful in the rodeo arena. And exactly why he was such an idiot when it came to relationships.

Ginger, who'd been standing in the back watching the show, gasped. The whole bar turned silent. Addison looked at him as if he'd grown two heads, Bob cursed under his breath and Carter cautiously set down the glass he was drying.

And suddenly the reality of what he'd just gotten himself into slapped him solidly in the face.

He'd essentially told the whole town that he was going to marry Jolene Arnold. All without doing her the honor of asking her opinion on the matter.

Addison looked three kinds of hurt. "Trent, is Jolene's baby yours?"

Without those test results, Trent wasn't ready to go there, so he went all macho. "Don't say her name again."

"But—"

Bob had had enough. "Addison, I sure appreciate your business, but I've had enough of your company here today."

"What?"

"You need to get on out of here. Now."

"You throwing me out, Bob?"

"I'm not throwing you out…yet," he replied, his voice all rough and gruff. "Right now you can still come back. Another day."

Trent folded his arms across his chest and glared. Lord, but he wanted to wipe that man's smirk off his face. Instinct told him that the only thing worse than speaking words that couldn't be taken back…was causing a scene.

After a moment's pause, Addison got up and left.

Trent went back to his burger.

Without saying a word, Carter poured him a draft and set it next to his plate. Trent sipped gratefully.

Then Bob pulled up a stool next to him. "What the hell you doing, Trent?"

"I'm sipping your draft."

"You know what I'm talking about. You can't start making up engagements at the drop of a hat."

Trent was past the point of no return. The only way to go was forward. And, actually, it didn't feel all that bad of a place to be. He cared about Jolene. And, well, since being a proper family was almost a reality what he was talking about made perfect sense. "I'm not making up a thing."

"So you've got nuptials planned with Jolene?"

"That's what I said, wasn't it?" he countered, not even cracking a smile. "I feel extremely lucky and blessed that she agreed to take me on."

"You stopping the rodeo circuit?" Carter asked.

"Hell, no. After New Year's, I'll get on my way."

"And Jo?"

"Jolene will stay here at home and take care of Amanda," he said easily.

But instead of looking pleased, Bob just shook his head. "I hope you know what you're doing."

Well, he didn't. That was a given. "If you could, try to sound a little happier when you see Jo. Otherwise you'll make her feel bad."

"Trent…"

"I'd love to stay and chat for a while, but to tell you the truth, I've got a mare who needs some attention."

"A mare," Bob echoed.

"She's got a rock in her shoe. Painful." Throwing a

twenty on the counter, he slipped on his coat and strode outside. As his brain started clicking, he thought of one thing, and one thing only. He had to get ahold of Jolene. Right away.

Because chances were very good that when she came in, talk of her engagement was going to slam her in the face.

His needed to be the first call she got. The moment the cold air hit his cheeks, he pulled out his cell and sent Jolene a text.

I just told everyone we're engaged, he typed and pressed Send.

Then, thinking some more, he figured more of an explanation was in order. Carefully, he typed some more. *Don't panic. I'll explain everything soon. I'll call you soon.*

He thought some more. Yep, that sounded pretty good.

Well, until he considered the possibility that Addison or Carter or Bob or somebody was going to get it into their head to do a little investigative work.

Thinking quickly, he added, *Whatever you do, don't talk to anyone else.*

As he got in his truck, he hoped to God she was in the mind to listen.

Chapter Twenty-One

It had been four minutes since Trent had sent her his series of asinine, cryptic text messages. Jolene knew that because she'd been watching the digital clock glow red on her oven, and tapping her toe as each second went by.

That was her main way to pass the time. Well, that, and contemplating the number of ways she could wring his neck.

Straightaway, another number clicked on. It was now five minutes since he'd sent the text.

Finally, her cell phone flickered, illuminating the number of the incoming call. The one she'd been waiting four minutes and twenty-three seconds for.

She snatched it up. "What the heck are you doing, Trent?"

"Driving. Can I come over?"

Though she'd also been listening for his knock, she changed her mind. "I don't think so." For the sake of his neck, she knew it would be best to keep a little space between them. Otherwise she was going to wring it good.

"Jolene? Come on. We need to talk."

"We can do that over the phone."

"Jo—"

"I'm serious, cowboy." There was no way she was dealing with him, face-to-face. Her emotions were too raw.

Every defense she'd built up to be around him was falling at too fast a rate. If he was standing there in front of her, with his too-blue eyes and his too-perfect body, well, there was no telling what she might find herself agreeing to.

"Well, will you at least listen to me?"

"Don't you think you ought to wait until you get off the road? Things are sketchy out there."

"That might be a real good idea," he said. "Um, just don't speak with anyone else until I get home, all right?"

"All right." She hung up fast, then. Her mind was spinning.

A chill ran down her spine as she contemplated even the idea of marrying him.

If they did get hitched, she'd be wed to a man she trusted. Pretty much the only man she'd ever trusted. More important she'd be married to Amanda Rose's daddy. They'd be a real family—just like in her dreams. But Jolene knew the reality was that Trent only came up with this crazy scheme because of Amanda. Not because he loved her. And that turned her dream to a nightmare.

Ten minutes later, there was a knock at her door almost in unison with her cell phone ringing again.

The number on the phone confirmed it was Trent, so she answered that first. "Are you knocking on my door?"

"No. I'm at home. Who's there?"

"I don't know," she said, as the knocking came again.

"I better go check." Two strides to the door, and one eye to the peephole showed that her visitor was Addison.

"Who is it?" Trent asked.

"Addison." She peeked again.

"Don't answer it!" Trent shouted in her ear.

Addison knocked again, a little more firmly this time.

"Why shouldn't I? Honestly, Trent, I think you've gone off the deep end. Hold on."

Putting the cell against her chest, she opened the door.

Addison greeted her with a pained expression. "Is it true?"

Oh, Lord. She really should have listened to Trent. "I can't talk now."

He braced a hand on the door frame. "Just tell me."

"Well…" Against her chest, her phone vibrated. Behind her, Amanda Rose started to fuss. "I really can't talk now," she hedged, because she couldn't deal with him.

"Jolene—"

"I mean it," she said, then proceeded to close the door on the poor guy's face.

"Jo?" Trent blurted so loudly, he could be in the room, too.

Putting the phone to her ear, she said, "Let me call you back. Amanda needs me."

"Hold on!" he said quickly. When she paused, he added, "I'll wait."

Amanda's whimpers morphed into star quality cries. "Trent, it may be a while…"

"I don't care. Just don't hang up. I don't mind waiting on Amanda."

"Are you sure?"

"Positive. Jolene, we need to talk. I drove home only because you insisted on it." He paused. "I'm going to have to get used to her fussing anyway, don't you think?"

Talk like that made him sound as if he actually did want to marry her. That, of course, was ludicrous.

But the thought did still make her become more compliant. "Maybe. Hold on, then." She set the phone down and neatly carried Amanda to her changing table. In no time at all, the sweetheart had her diaper changed and was dressed in a fresh romper.

As she carried Amanda to the kitchen for a bottle, Trent started talking again. "Is Addison gone?"

"Yes. Now are you going to tell me what's been going on?"

SITTING IN HIS FATHER'S study, the smell of tobacco and leather strong, Trent leaned back in his father's chair and tried to come up with a suitable reply. Jolene deserved an answer. A good answer, too.

But he wasn't sure he was going to be able to give her one.

He decided to go for honesty, even though he had a feeling that the God's honest truth was going to be more than a little of a letdown.

"Jolene, the truth is, I was sitting in Bob's this afternoon, eating a burger and trying to get warm, when Addison started talking about you."

"And that made you suddenly insane?"

"Just give me a sec. I'm trying…" He paused. Already, his blood was heating up again. Just thinking about how Addison had been talking about her made him twitchy. "Fact is, Addison was talking about you something awful."

To his surprise, she chuckled. "That's what set you off? Trent, your concern is sweet, but you shouldn't have let his words bother you."

"What are you talking about? Jolene, he likes you, and he was wanting Carter to talk about you, too." Even as his words left his mouth, Trent was horrified. Could he sound any more eighth grade?

"I know he likes me."

"He was talking about Amanda's daddy. Speculating…"

"You mean you?" she asked drily. Before he could respond to that, she sighed. "What he's saying is no different than anything other people have said."

He shook his head in dismay, then realized that of course she couldn't see him. "That's no excuse. He shouldn't have been talking about your problems in a bar."

"All my life, people have been talking about me. Making sure I knew that I wasn't worth much."

"That's not true."

"That's not true for *you*," she corrected. "But, the plain and simple truth is, even my daddy didn't think much of me."

Her daddy had been a drunken SOB. "Jolene," he murmured. "Honey…"

"Let me finish, Trent." He could hear her swallow while she tried to regain her composure. "My daddy used to tell me that I wasn't too smart, and that my looks weren't too special, either. He made me think that the only way I was going to get anyone to ever pay attention to me was in bad ways. So I was a little too loud in crowds. I developed an attitude that came across as one hundred percent I Don't Give A Damn. And I learned that if I smiled at men, and if I flirted every now and then, sometimes I wouldn't be alone at night." She lowered her voice. "And sometimes, I wouldn't even feel so bad about myself."

Her words broke his heart. And he realized that now it wasn't just testosterone pushing him toward nuptials. It was his feelings for her.

They'd been buried down deep but they'd taken root, sometime when he'd been four or five or six. Sometime when they'd been together, Trent had realized that Jolene was special.

Special to him.

"Trent? Have I completely shocked you?"

He cleared his throat. "Not at all."

"Well…good. Anyway, so you see, there's no reason to worry about Addison talking about me."

There, in his dad's office, Trent got to his feet. While he wished he was standing face-to-face with her, he decided perhaps it was for the best, the two of them being in different places at the moment. He needed every one of his father's influences around him when he said the next words.

"I don't want there to be another day in your life when you feel you have to listen to talk like that," he said. "Jolene, I want you to marry me. I want us to be a couple."

"What about Amanda?"

"You said she was mine."

"What about the test results? Don't you want to wait for them?"

"You said that was just a formality." When he heard

her sigh, he started talking as if his life depended on it. "Jo, I really do think we need to do this."

"Because?"

"Because I know we'll be good together. I know we can get along just fine." Encouraged by her silence, he started talking faster. "And, well, I feel like a snake even mentioning this, but I have to say that we can have good sex, too."

"Oh, Trent."

"Was that not a compliment?" He scratched his head. "Great sex?"

"Even great sex isn't enough."

"I'll take care of you, Jolene. I'll take care of you and Amanda, even though you say you don't need to be taken care of."

"I don't need your money. I'm doing fine…"

"Okay, how's this? How about never again are you going to have to feel like you're alone. Like it's you against the world."

When she softly gasped, Trent closed his eyes. He knew he'd found her weak spot. Jolene was a tough cookie, but she was sweet natured and sometimes fragile, too.

And all her life, she'd basically been fending for herself. "Come on, Jo," he said softly.

"But we don't love each other."

"Do we really need that?" he asked. "I've been around, Jolene. I've known a lot of women, and I've known a lot of couples. I've met men so 'in love' with the gal he's sleeping with that he does one dumb thing after another. And two weeks later, he hates the girl."

After a pause, she murmured, "I've known couples like that, too."

He'd heard it. He'd heard that tinge of surprise and commitment in her voice.

He grinned. He was going to get her to agree.

"Jolene, Amanda needs a father. And even more important than that, you need me."

"But what about you? I don't want you to regret this."

"I think I need you, too. I'm not going to regret it."

"You might. One day, you might meet some gal. Some pretty, ladylike gal."

"Jolene, honey. I don't want a gal like that," he countered, realizing all of a sudden that he meant every word.

"Trent, maybe she'll have gone to good schools and be on the social register. Maybe she'll be worth waiting for. And…and, you'll be stuck with me."

"That's not going to happen. Because I will be proud to have you. I will be proud and happy to call you my wife. And call Amanda Rose my daughter." Because he knew she was just seconds from saying yes, he added, "Come on. Sure you could tell me no, just to prove a point. But I'm going to keep asking, and I know in my heart that you're eventually gonna say yes. Let's save all that angst and heartbreak and do this now."

"Yes," she said quickly.

"Yes, to getting married? Are you sure? Because once you say yes to me, I'm not going to let you back out of it."

"I won't back out."

"Jo, if you could see me now, you'd know my grin couldn't get any wider. Thank you. You've made me so very happy."

After a pause, she said, "You've made me happy, too."

He leaned his head against the wall. "Let's get married soon."

"How soon?"

"Like today. Or tomorrow," he said in a rush. "Yeah. I think that would be the right thing. The best thing. We ought to go take care of things tomorrow, so we can be settled in and happy, all before Christmas."

"Trent—Lord have mercy... There's no reason to rush, is there?"

"I think so. Please, honey? We can get married, and put up a tree. It will be fun."

"What about licenses and all that?"

"I'll take care of it. Tomorrow morning? Can I pick you up then and we'll go do it?"

"Sure." Her voice sounded all squidgy and dazed. "Oh, Trent, I can hardly think."

"Think about being Jolene Riddell," he said. "Think about that all day and night. If you do that, you won't need to worry about another thing."

"I'll do it," she whispered.

He wanted the words. "Is that a yes?"

"Yes."

"You made me very happy, Jolene." With surprise, he realized he meant that, too.

"I, uh, need to feed Amanda now."

"I'll call you later. Goodbye, sweetheart."

After he hung up, he breathed deep. He'd done it. He was going to marry Jolene Arnold.

His family was going to be shocked and surprised. Maybe even a little disappointed that they hadn't been informed before the fact.

But all he had to do was remember her little speech.

To remember how nobody in her world had loved her enough to put her first.

And how the voice inside of him had whispered that he wanted to be the person who did that. Not Addison. Not some other man down the road.

He wanted to be the man in her life.

And that's when he knew, without a doubt, that he'd done the right thing.

Chapter Twenty-Two

"I promise, you're going to love this place," Trent told Jolene as they walked across the parking lot to the Golden Dove, Electra's lone fine dining establishment.

"I can't wait to try it," Jolene said, but inside, her stomach was a mess of knots. Though she appreciated Trent wanting to give her a special wedding dinner, it would have been just fine with her to have gone home and eaten a frozen pizza.

She might have preferred it.

Trent held the door open for her, then strode forward with a big grin. Jolene followed far more slowly, taking in the heavy garland adorning each doorway, and the beautiful crystal vases holding gold and cranberry colored Christmas balls.

The whole place looked like a Christmas scene out of an expensive magazine. She felt a bit like Dorothy, plopped right in the middle of it.

"Hey, Jean Claude," Trent said to a very dapper, somewhat cosmopolitan-looking man watching them approach. "It's good to see you."

"Oh, Mr. Riddell, what a nice surprise. It's been too long since you've stopped by."

"It sure has." Jolene watched her brand-new husband

reach out and shake Jean Claude's hand. "But it comes with the territory, I guess. I can't be here and ride bulls, too."

"Our loss is rodeo's gain." Then he turned expectantly Jolene's way...and she felt on display.

Trent curved a hand around her elbow. "Jean Claude, please meet Jolene. Jolene, honey, this is Jean Claude Valentine. He owns this establishment. He's also the resident foodie of North Texas and recent guest on the Food Network."

He gave a little bow. "It's a pleasure, Miss."

Miss. Jolene smiled, but inside, her heart skipped a beat as she nervously looked Trent's way. He hadn't introduced her as his wife. Was he embarrassed of her already?

As if he'd read her mind, Trent added, "She's not a Miss anymore, Jean Claude." Looking pleased as punch, he glanced her way fondly. "Jolene and I got married today."

The man's eyes grew round as he took in Trent's black suit and her ivory sheath dress. "Did you two just come from your wedding?"

Feeling as though giant butterflies were fluttering in her stomach, Jolene said, "Actually, we just came from the justice of the peace."

"Congratulations, my dear!" He took her hand and kissed her knuckles. "Congratulations to you both. We're going to need to make tonight extra special, yes?"

As Jolene watched in wonder, Jean Claude snapped his fingers, called over a waiter and whispered into his ear. Then he turned to Trent. "Allen will have a table ready for you in just a moment."

"We're in no hurry. Are we, sugar?" Trent asked.

Jolene shook her head. No, she was in too much of a daze to do much besides concentrate on the present. Otherwise, the past twenty-four hours would feel as if they were in someone else's life.

Moments after she'd said yes, Jolene had sat, shell-shocked, when she'd heard another knock at her door. Steeling herself to finally deal with Addison, she'd been stunned to see her friend Cheryl instead, who'd walked right in like she'd owned the place.

"Tell me everything I've heard isn't a lie," Cheryl blurted.

"It depends what you've heard. Did you hear that Trent and I are getting married tomorrow?"

"Oh. My. Gosh."

Jolene had smiled, shrugged, then promptly burst into tears. "I don't know what to do."

"Are you happy about it?"

"Very."

"Then that's all I need to know." From then on, Cheryl had taken charge. She'd answered the phone that had suddenly started ringing off the hook. When Bob called, she filled him in before passing the receiver to Jolene.

In addition, Cheryl discussed details with Trent, fixed Jolene an omelet and inspected her closet and drawers.

The whole time, Jolene sat with Amanda and enjoyed the sensation of letting someone else be in charge.

An hour after that, the three of them had braved the weather and had gone to Amarillo to find Jolene a bridal dress.

Late last night, Jolene had picked up the phone and

called Bob again. Though she'd already told him she was going to take time off, she wanted to make sure he was okay with it.

"I'm more than okay," he ended up saying. "You and Trent are a good match."

"I hope I'm doing the right thing."

"You are. I saw something in Trent's eyes when Addison was talking about you. Trent cares about you, Jo. Don't ever forget that."

When she'd hung up, she'd finally felt at peace.

This morning, Cheryl came over with Dwayne to watch Amanda Rose. When Jolene had wanted to offer more and more babysitting instructions, Cheryl had assured her everything would be just fine. And then she'd waved Jolene off when Trent had picked her up.

Now she and Trent were having twenty-four hours of alone time. And it felt strange and awkward and wonderful, too.

Trent rested a hand on the middle of her back, returning her to the present. "It's all right, you know," he murmured, leaning in close. "I know it feels like we're doing something crazy, but I've got a good feeling about us."

Secretly, she felt the same way. It was so right to be married to Amanda's daddy. And it was so right to be married to the man she'd first loved at six years old.

"Being married to you feels right. I'm just not so sure about the restaurant. It looks too fancy for me."

"This? Oh, you're going to like it here. I promise. The food's great."

The waiter who Jean Claude had asked to prepare a table approached, a couple menus in his hands. "If you two would follow me?"

Trent gestured for Jolene to go first.

Each table was covered in white linen and had little gold lamps and holly in the center. Just about every table was occupied. She felt more than one person's gaze on her as they walked through the maze of tables and chairs. Not trusting herself, she looked straight ahead and tried to remember that her ivory dress was pretty, and classy-looking, too.

When they got to a corner table, next to the windows on one side, Jolene sat in the chair the man pulled out, then gazed at Trent as he took the seat across from her.

After presenting Trent with a menu, the man left. And Jolene heaved a sigh of relief.

Reaching out, Trent took her hand in his and linked their fingers. "You look pretty, Jolene. Have I told you that lately?"

She couldn't help but smile. "You've been telling me that all day."

"Well, you do. Better than that. You look like a very beautiful bride."

Jolene scanned his face. She couldn't find a bit of doubt there. Maybe, just maybe, he really did want to be with her. And that the two of them were meant to be married.

"You're lookin' very fine, too."

"I tried." He flashed a smile. "Now, you order whatever you want, we'll enjoy ourselves, then get on home."

Bam! All thoughts of food and fancy restaurants disappeared in an instant. But she couldn't afford to push this experience away. Especially not if Trent was enjoying himself so much.

Keeping her voice light, she murmured, "What's good here?"

"Everything."

She scanned the menu. Noticed the entrée items included duck and veal and steak and lobster. "It's been a while since I've eaten out. I've forgotten how to be spoiled."

His expression turned serious. "Jo, sometimes, I don't think anyone's ever spoiled you. But that will change. I guarantee it."

He sounded so certain, Jolene pushed her worries aside.

When their waiter approached, Trent ordered a bottle of wine, Steak Diane and Trout Almandine. And started teasing her, making her smile.

She responded in kind. And soon, all the awkwardness faded and next thing she knew, Jolene was telling Trent all kinds of stories about customers at Bob's, including which couples regularly came in together but left with other dates.

In turn, Trent told her about life on the road, and a few stories about Ginny.

The moment their dinner plates were whisked away, Jean Claude approached with the most beautiful white cake Jolene had ever seen. The ivory icing was in swirls around the edges, and white chocolate shavings decorated the center. Red roses were intertwined and placed around the plate.

Trent quirked an eyebrow at Jean Claude. "You just whipped us up a wedding cake."

"But of course. Everyone needs a wedding cake," he said, smiling around at the rest of the restaurant.

That's when Jolene realized that the whole crowd was completely intent on them.

A man two tables over whispered low. "Is this your wedding day, Trent?"

Looking Jolene's way, he smiled. "It's our wedding day. Mine and Jolene's."

For a split second, Jolene was afraid someone was going to tell him he was out of his mind. That he should have chosen better.

But instead, words of congratulations and applause rang out.

Jean Claude beamed. "Everyone, please join me in a toast to Mr. and Mrs. Trent Riddell."

"Champagne for everyone," Trent called out.

Laughter and applause filled the room.

Jolene looked around, expecting the majority of the people to be looking at her in disapproval. But instead of seeing glares of contempt, she saw only expressions of happiness.

She felt her eyes prick with tears.

As people started approaching them, Trent stood up and helped her to her feet. With extreme patience, he thanked each person, and introduced her to them.

Corks popped, champagne was poured and more toasts were given. In the middle of it all, Jean Claude pulled out a camera, taking pictures of the two of them sitting together, and in front of their cake.

Then finally, their cake was sliced and with a bit of goading from the crowd, Jolene lifted her fork to his lips. Slowly he opened his mouth, and she fed him his first bite. But not before he licked her fingers.

Someone whistled low.

But Jolene wasn't really sure who. Because with that

one swipe of his tongue, she felt as if she was on fire. And suddenly nothing else mattered but being alone with Trent Riddell.

"JOLENE, I HAVE TO SAY IT," Trent said as he drove out of the parking lot. "I love being with you, but I feel like my arm is missing. I don't want to be without Amanda. Would you mind terribly if we went and got her?"

She breathed a sigh of relief. Though her trout had been amazing and the cake had been as delicious as it looked, there'd been a constant, nagging feeling of guilt, too. She was Amanda's mommy, and having someone else take care of her when she wasn't working made her feel really bad. "I don't mind at all. I've been feeling the same way."

"You should have said something."

"I didn't want to spoil things."

"Jo."

"Well, you went to all that trouble to plan things out with Cheryl. And I did love our fancy dinner, Trent. It wouldn't have been the same with a baby in tow."

"But we're done now, right?"

"I'm going to always remember being there. Thank you for taking me to somewhere so nice."

He looked at her strangely in the dim light. "You make it sound like you're never going to eat there again. We can go back whenever you want."

"It was really expensive."

"That's nothing you need to worry about anymore, sugar." Looking at her in an almost tender way, he said, "I'll tell you what. Let's go back next week, and we'll bring Miss Amanda."

"You can't bring a baby there."

"Sure we can. Everyone's going to love her."

His enthusiasm startled a laugh from her. "If that's what you want."

"It is. And I always get what I want." He waited a beat. "Right now I want to go pick up Amanda. You okay with that?"

"I'm not going to be the girl who stands in between Trent Riddell with what he wants."

"Now you're learning," he said with a grin. "Sometimes it's best just to let me have my way. Especially when I'm right."

Suddenly, she felt like his wife. His partner. Gripping his arm, she said, "You might have to learn a few things, too, Trent. Just to let you know."

The chuckle that filled the cab of the truck filled her heart, too. And gave her a sense of optimism she hadn't known existed.

Chapter Twenty-Three

Later that night, standing in the corner of Amanda's room, Jolene watched her baby sleep. Hoping her daughter's sweet, even breathing would calm her nerves.

But this time, even her baby's slumber couldn't ease her. Fact was, she felt as if her skin was on fire. She was nervous. Real nervous.

Which was silly, of course. She and Trent weren't going to do anything that they hadn't done before.

So why was she anxious about getting into bed with Trent again? Was it because this time they were actually going to be in bed, instead of her floor?

Because they were sober, not three sheets to the wind?

No. The truth was much more scary. She was his wife now. This would be the first of many times.

And this time, unlike so many others, this time it meant a whole lot more than simple infatuation. Now, real emotions were involved. She didn't just love him, she was completely *in* love with him. And somehow that little word made all the difference in the world.

Oh, she knew Trent probably didn't feel that way. Maybe he never would. Though she knew he cared for her, and he felt a true sense of compassion for her situation, Jolene knew he didn't love her.

Just as she was completely certain that she loved him. 'Course, that wasn't all that hard to understand. He was a gorgeous man. He was famous and just bad enough to excite a woman's blood. And he was rich.

But none of that really mattered to her, not really. The fact was, she'd loved Trent Riddell, in one form or another, for pretty much all her life.

He'd been her stability when she was small, giving her his friendship and his family. After the Riddells had moved up and her family had moved away and things had gotten even worse, Jolene had hugged those memories close. It was because of his parents that Jolene had known that the way her mother and father behaved wasn't the only way to be.

Funny how life happened.

Just a year ago, they'd shared a night together. Sure, it had involved too much drinking and not enough common sense. But there had also been real fondness there. Affection.

And honest to God passion.

And, of course, he'd given her a baby that she loved more than her life.

What she needed to do now was push all her doubts away and go to him. She needed to put on a smile and make him glad she was in his bed.

That, she could do. If she was brave enough.

"Jolene?" Trent appeared at the doorway, arms crossed over his bare chest. Below, he was wearing a pair of flannel pajama bottoms with reindeers on them. The ties were hanging out at the waistband.

He looked adorable, which eased her nerves. "I never thought I'd live to see you dressed up in reindeer."

"Huh?" He looked down and grinned. "These are from my sister-in-law, Susan, if you can believe it. We had our family Christmas before they left."

His family Christmas.

That she was now a part of. As she was digesting that, Trent tilted his head to one side, studying her. Little by little, his gaze went from searching to something darker.

Something more hot-blooded.

She shivered in response.

Keeping his voice down, he said, "Amanda looks like she's just fine."

"I think so."

"So…are you planning to stay in here much longer?"

She shook her head. "I was just, you know, watching her sleep."

Pure tenderness drifted over his features as he glanced toward Amanda, sleeping on her stomach, her legs curled up under her, butt in the air. "She is pretty much the sweetest thing I've ever seen."

That made her happy.

"But at the moment, I was thinking that I'd much rather be looking at someone else in bed."

Jolted, she met his gaze.

He seemed to understand what she was thinking. Even if she didn't understand herself anymore. His gaze flickered over her, over the glistening white satin nightgown that Cheryl had bought for her—even though Jolene had blushed at the thought of wearing white into the bedroom.

But to her surprise, Trent wasn't teasing her about

the virginal gown. Instead, a fire lit his eyes, making the blue irises look almost purple. Smoky.

"I want you in my bed," he murmured when they walked out into the hall. "I want to wrap my arms around you and hold you close."

Her mouth went dry.

How did he know? How did he know that those were the words she couldn't ignore? Never had a man said such things to her. They'd talked about her ass. They'd told her she was pretty. They'd praised her long legs.

But no one had ever talked to her as though she was worth more than the sum of her parts. Mesmerized, she stepped toward him. As she walked, she watched his gaze skim her body and pause at her breasts, slide down the satin to the shadow at the junction of her thighs.

And for the first time in a long while, she was thankful that she was pretty. That she had a body men liked to see.

She stepped closer. As if he couldn't stop himself from touching her, one hand reached out and cupped her hip.

Lifting her chin, she raised her eyebrows. And, going on instinct alone, offered a challenge. "Is that all you want, Trent? You only want to hold me?"

"Hell, no." He brushed back a curl over her shoulder. "I want a whole lot more than that." Leaning in, he pressed his lips against her neck. "I want you, Jolene. You're more than gorgeous," he murmured, sending a bolt of desire through her.

His eyes darkened as he traced a line along her collar bone. "Fact is, I've seen little in my life that's as sexy as you in white satin." A muscle in his cheek jumped.

"But I'm willing to settle for just holding. If, ah…if that's all you want."

He was giving her a choice. She felt his gentle touch all the way through her. She knew she'd never forget his words, and the way they made her feel.

So wanted.

And though everything inside of her practically was itching to throw out a sassy remark and just do what was expected of her, she realized that Trent wasn't teasing her at all.

"I want to make love with you," she said slowly. Then smiled when pure delight entered his eyes.

"I'm so glad you said that," he drawled before kissing her. He took her breath away with his touch. The way his lips, so warm, so tender, brushed against hers, nibbled her bottom lip.

Two fingers traced the line from her shoulder, down her arm, until their fingers linked. He stepped closer.

Unable to help herself, she pressed against him, felt his sharp intake of air, felt his erection harden.

Clasping her hand, he tugged her down the hall and up the stairs. Jolene skimmed her hand along the garland, enjoying the faint scent of pine as they paused at the landing, then continued up the stairs and into his bedroom.

"Finally," he said when they stepped inside. "Now come here and kiss me."

Without hesitation, Jolene walked into his arms. The moment their lips met, things turned passionate. Trent's hands ran over her body like a blind man.

A very adept, impatient blind man.

She stepped back, and he looked at her curiously. "You're not gonna turn shy on me, are you?"

She had to smile at that. "I don't know if I've ever been shy. Just, let's slow down a little. Do you mind?"

"Never," he said against her lips as he nibbled, then plundered, and then, just as he promised, he turned languid and sweet, taking his time, encouraging her to explore.

She wrapped her arms around his neck and kissed him for all he was worth. Oh, it was so easy.

Soon, her arms curved up around his shoulders, and Trent's hands slipped around her waist. And then their mouths met again.

Her feelings might have been tentative, but her body knew what it wanted. Their mouths opened, and before she really thought too much about it, Trent was running his hands along her nightgown, watching the satin shimmer and shift under his fingers. His eyes lit up when her nipples puckered under his touch. She was about to suggest that she pull the gown off, when he slipped her straps off her shoulders and eased the fabric down.

Like a waterfall, it slipped down her body, ending in a pool at her feet.

Now standing only in a white lace thong—again, the brainchild of Cheryl—she lifted her chin.

He grinned. "I am the luckiest man on the face of the earth."

She wasted no time in rubbing a finger along the soft waistband of his pajamas, then pulled down those dancing reindeer.

Eager hands slid off the last of her lace. And then, well, there they were.

Standing in front of each other, looking, exploring. After a few minutes, Trent surprised her by gathering her close and pressing his lips to her neck. "You're a pretty thing, Jolene. You are the most beautiful woman I've ever seen." He raised his face to hers. "But, of course, you always were."

With a wry smile she said, "My body's changed some. Having a baby will do that."

"Uh-huh," he said between long, openmouthed kisses. "Your body is perfect. You're perfect. You can't be any more perfect."

She sighed in anticipation as he gathered her close and curved her hands around his waist, loving every touch, loving his words.

"Jo, honey...you ready to check out my very pretty bed?"

There was only one answer. "I thought you'd never ask."

And then, like a prince in a fairy tale, Trent picked her up and deposited her on his bed. She didn't have to wait long before she was lying underneath him, and his lips were exploring her breasts. And his right hand—oh, that hand!—had remembered to touch her in just the way she liked.

As Jolene curved her thighs around his hips, as he entered her and she felt that rush of pleasure only he seemed to make her feel, she was aware that neither of them had mentioned love.

But there was still love there.

It was in the way Trent kissed her so sweetly. It was in the way he waited...and waited...and waited until she was satisfied. It was in the way she held him to her and wrapped her arms around him and called out his name when they climaxed.

And in the way Trent did exactly what he had said

he would do—he curled up next to Jolene and held her close.

And she fell asleep in his arms. Finally a wife. But more important, finally feeling like she was wanted... and where she needed to be.

And that's when she knew she'd been incredibly wrong. What she'd done with Trent, she'd never done before. She'd never made love before. She'd never been held close like this before.

She'd never felt so comforted and special before.

What was happening between them? Why, it was all brand-new.

Chapter Twenty-Four

The night before, sleep hadn't been on the program. After making love once, they'd both decided that once wasn't enough.

Twice hadn't been, either.

Then, around five in the morning, Amanda started fussing and squirming and fussing some more. Jolene got up to take care of her.

And then Trent got up, eager to take care of Jolene. It was his job to look out for her, he decided, as he watched Jolene tenderly coax the baby to take a sip from her bottle. She needed someone to lean on, and he was ready to be that person.

He rubbed Jo's back as he watched her cuddle Amanda and was struck by how Jolene's patience never seemed to end.

"Do you think she's going to be all right?" he asked an hour later, when they'd come back to Amanda's room and Jolene had laid her back in her Pack 'N Play.

"She's gonna be fine," Jolene said with a faint smile. "At the moment, I think she's on a little power trip. Look at her! She's on her back, wiggling around. It's only when I pick her up to try and rock her that she gets irritable."

"You think that's it? All she wants is to move around a bit?"

"Uh-huh…" She sat on the end of the guest bedroom bed. "But I should probably sit in here, just to be sure."

Seeing Jolene on a brand-new bed gave Trent ideas. "If we're stuck in here, we might as well roll around, too, don't you think?"

"Trent, you're incorrigible." Her voice was firm, but her eyes were full of humor. And invitation.

"Only with you," he murmured, kissing her.

And as Trent remembered just how sweet she'd tasted last night, just how perfect she'd felt pressed up against him, he pulled her close and opened his mouth.

Right as his cell phone began to ring.

"I better get that," he murmured when he saw it was Jarred. "Hey, what's up?"

"Nothing. I just wanted to check in early, since I knew you'd be getting up with the horses."

He winked Jolene's way. "Everything's good here. How's your trip?"

"We're having a good time. Serena's about to run me ragged, though. She's decided she likes roller coasters in the dark. We've been on Space Mountain three times."

Trent leaned back against the headboard and motioned for Jolene to cuddle next to him. "That's good to hear."

"How are things going there?"

"Things?" He looked at Jolene again and smiled. "Things are fine."

"Anything new?"

He was about to answer when Amanda fussed again. As Jolene moved to pick her up, Trent contemplated how to tell his family the big news. "Quite a bit."

"What's going on? And what's that noise in the background? It sounds like a baby."

Perhaps that would be the way to get to the truth. "It sounds like a baby because it is a baby. Jolene and Amanda are here."

"Trent? What's going on?"

He cleared his throat. When he spied Jolene looking at him as if she was afraid he was going to pretend she didn't exist, he winked. Then took a deep breath and plunged off the cliff. "We got married yesterday."

"What?"

"You heard me." Warily, Trent cast a look in Jolene's direction. His brand-new wife was acting as if his conversation wasn't bothering her none, but he was beginning to realize that she was a pretty darn good actress.

Actually, over the years, she must have learned a heck of a lot of skills, learned to look as though nothing mattered to her.

But now he was smarter, at least when it came to Jolene. He figured all that sass she displayed in the bar at Bob's was mostly an act.

"Trent, how about we come on home?" Jarred asked too carefully, as if he was afraid his little brother had officially lost his mind.

"We?"

"If you ran off and got married without letting us know, I think you need a lot more help than only I can give you."

Having all of them there was the absolutely last thing they needed. "There's no call for that."

"There is if you're marrying someone like Jolene."

Trent's voice hardened. "I'm really going to hope and pray that I just heard you wrong."

"You didn't." Though Jarred must have covered the receiver of his phone, Trent still heard him curse. "I'm going to talk to everyone and call you back."

"No. You don't need to do that. And, I don't need you to come out here." Behind him, he heard Jolene gasp. He pivoted again and tried to soothe her worries with a little wave of three fingers.

But he wasn't doing too good of a job from the look on her face. "It's okay," he mouthed.

As hope filled her gaze, his brother started spouting off again in his ear. "You obviously do. You've gone loco, brother. I don't know what happened. Shoot, maybe that concussion you got from Diablo was way worse than you let on...but either way—"

"Jarred, you're rambling," he interrupted, taking great care to make his voice soft and slow.

"I am not!"

"You'd best stop yelling in my ear. You're going to make me go deaf. Then I really won't be worth nothing."

"Trent!"

"I'm gonna hang up if you don't settle," he said patiently.

After a long pause, Jarred spoke again. "I've settled."

"You sure?"

"Positive. Now, when did this...this marriage happen?" his brother asked, far more quietly.

"Yesterday. We went to the courthouse and got it done." Getting up, Trent walked over to the end of the bed and kissed Jolene's worried brow. When it smoothed a bit, he brushed his lips against her cheek. "It was nice," he said with a smile. Still looking at her, he said, "And then we went to the Golden Dove and ate."

After a lengthy pause, Jarred bit out, "All because you got that girl pregnant?"

"Watch your mouth, Jarred." Trent's temper was hardly checked before he moved away from Jolene and walked to his father's study.

"Trent?" Jolene stood up. "Is everything okay?"

Lord, but he was messing everything up. "You hold on," he told his brother. Then after he set down the phone, he turned on his heel and walked back to Jolene, taking her hand and giving it a gentle squeeze. "Everything's great," he lied. "Jarred's just a little excited."

"He's more than that. I can hear him yelling on the phone."

"He always did have a hard time keeping his voice under control. Come to think of it, he might be deaf in one ear," he said in a rush. "Anyway, honey, you stay here. I'm going to go talk to him. He'll calm down soon. I promise."

"And if he doesn't?"

Trent had never felt more like his own man. "If he doesn't, it don't matter none," he said with certainty. "All that does matter is that you're my wife. We're a couple now."

She still looked skeptical, which was to be expected, because she was a lot of things, but she was no fool. "But, Trent—"

"Jo, honey, let me go. If I don't pick up soon, he's going to hang up and I'm gonna have to call him back. But please don't worry. When I get off the phone, we're going to decorate a tree. We're going to have a nice rest of our day. No phone call is going to ruin it. I promise."

"All right…"

"Good. Now I'll be back shortly," he assured her.

Two steps away, he picked up the receiver again. Once he got out of Jolene's view, he picked up the pace, got to his daddy's study, and closed the door behind him. "You there?"

"I am. And I couldn't help but hear your tender speech," Jarred said sarcastically.

"Jarred, you listen to me. I won't put up with you talking bad about her. She's my wife." And here was where he should mention that little thing about being Amanda's daddy.

But, like the coward he was, he didn't. Even though for the first time he wasn't fooling himself with lies about waiting for tests results.

"Hey, now—" Jarred said.

"I've never said a word against Serena. I'll never say a word against Susan. Those ladies are my brothers' wives," he said quietly. "I would've expected the same thing from you."

"Oh, come on. *Jolene Arnold* isn't the same—"

"She is," he bit out. "Jolene Arnold is Jolene Riddell. She is my wife and she will be forever."

"Are you going to explain yourself to me or do I need to go find Dad?"

"If you found Dad, he'd understand my reasons." The moment he said the words, Trent also realized that his dad would also approve of the marriage.

But Jarred did not. "What the heck is that supposed to mean?"

"Nothing I want to talk to you about right now."

"Listen. You will tell me what's going on so I can help you figure things out."

"Did I just step into a time warp? Because I could

have sworn that you were talking to me like I was fourteen years old. I don't have to explain myself to anyone."

"I'm just trying to understand."

"Okay. Here's the deal, Jarred. I've been spending time with Jo. She's got an adorable baby. I wanted her to be my wife."

"On the spur of the moment like that?"

He took a deep breath. "It's done, Jarred. I married her and she's my wife. And I don't really care to hear your opinions."

A long moment passed. "Do you want me to tell Dad and Cal? You know, smooth things out?"

"I don't need you smoothing anything. I can tell them myself."

After another pause, a new note entered his brother's voice. "You're not my kid brother anymore, are you?"

"I haven't been that kid for a very long time, Jarred. I've been living on my own for ten years, managing a career and getting the crap beat out of me on a regular basis by large farm animals. Did you really think all I did was party and wish I had y'all to tell me what to do?"

"I guess I did," Jarred said with a chuckle. "I'm sorry. What I said—" He cleared his throat. "What I said about Jolene, about your wife, it was uncalled for. Will you accept my apology?"

"Of course." But looking at the closed door, he knew it was time to get back to Jolene. She had to be going crazy by now. "But I will let you pass on my good news for me. I don't think I'm up for another one of these conversations."

"All right. I'll have them call you later."

"Do that." Still looking at the door, he said, "But you

better warn them not to call if they can't wish us well. Jolene's my wife now. And we've got a daughter." Relief rushed through him as he finally said the right thing.

"Next time I call, I'd be honored to speak to her and give her my best wishes."

"Next time you call, I'd be honored if you did that. But I think I better go. Jolene's going to be worried if I don't go back to her."

"Um, anything going on with the ranch you have concerns about? That really is why I called."

Trent knew a peace offering when he heard it. "Actually, yeah." Briefly he told Jarred about the inventory in the barn and some other discrepancies that Jolene had found.

"I'm surprised as hell to hear about all this. Why didn't you tell us when you first suspected?"

"Because I was afraid I was just too ignorant," he confessed. "I thought it was just another case of me not knowing what was going on…"

"And Cal and I probably would've both told you that," Jarred said with some regret. "I'm starting to realize that I haven't been giving you enough credit for much."

"You've given me credit. Usually it was more than I deserved. I haven't been here. And I did need this time to figure out things. But things are fine now. Fine," he repeated, hoping if he said it again he might actually believe it.

Now that things were back to normal, he brought up his earlier concern. "So about Pete? What do you want to do?"

"I'll talk to Cal and Dad, but I think I'll get on the phone and visit with Paul. He'll have some ideas."

"Paul as in Paul Carrington? The sheriff?"

"Uh-huh. But he's also Paul Carrington, the guy I went through school with. He's smart and he might have a sense of how to approach Pete."

Trent was grateful to let his brothers share the burden. Yes, he was his own man, but he was also part of a family. It felt good to finally reach out to his brothers without feeling as though he was incompetent. "Thanks. I appreciate that."

"Don't worry. We'll get things straightened out. Between the three of us and Dad, Pete won't stand a chance."

After he hung up, Trent sighed. Now all he had to do was figure out how in the world he was going to convince Jolene that everything was going to be okay.

Chapter Twenty-Five

When he walked into the living room, Trent looked as frazzled as she'd ever seen him. Lines she hadn't even known existed were surrounding his eyes and mouth.

All the hope that she'd been feeling when she woke up dissipated in an instant. His family was upset with him. They couldn't believe he'd married her.

And, shoot, how could they? Most likely he was regretting everything about them, regretting ever answering the door when she'd come calling.

Surely he regretted their marriage.

Well, she could fix this. Standing up in front of the couch, she pressed her hands together. "Hi."

"Hi." He grinned. "This is why we're going to be good together, Jo. I've been wondering how in the world I was going to be able to make up for that phone call... and here you are, already making everything better."

"I don't know if I can make things better with your family."

"You don't need to worry about that. You're my wife. Things are better, too. After explaining things to Jarred, he's real excited and anxious to talk to you."

Oh, she bet he was anxious! "I doubt that."

"You shouldn't. I'm telling you the truth." Stepping

closer, he sat down, then propped his feet up on the wide maple coffee table. "Now, come here and sit with me for a bit."

She did as he asked, tucking her feet under her thighs. But her heart was beating fast. "About Amanda, maybe we could call the lab. See if they got the official results yet…"

"You know what? I don't think I even care about those tests anymore."

But she figured he did. Until he heard the proof, there would always be a grain of doubt for him.

And she knew she couldn't compete with that for very long. "I think I'll still give them a call."

He cut off her words with a kiss. "Please don't worry so much, sugar," he murmured, his lips practically brushing against hers with every word. "Everything's going to be all right."

When he kissed her again, parting his lips and exploring her mouth with his tongue, she leaned close and kissed him back, loving the way he tasted. Would she ever get tired of the way he kissed? Or the way he liked to cup her jaw with one hand and gently caress her jaw with his thumb while he kissed her so slowly, making her toes tingle and her limbs go weak?

And just like that, she pushed her resolve to the side.

She leaned closer and pressed her hand to his chest, liking the way she could feel his muscles under the cool cotton of his shirt.

He pulled back slightly, glanced toward Amanda, who'd fallen asleep on a thick quilt on the other side of the room. "She finally gonna sleep for a while?"

"I think so."

"For how long, do you think?"

"At least an hour."

He grinned. "Hey, now. That's great news."

"And why is that?"

"'Cause I want some of her momma right now," he drawled, his eyes teasing, promising so much.

"You've got me," she said, because it was the truth, and there was really nothing else to say. She loved him. And for as long as he wanted her near, she was going to be his. At least until he didn't want her anymore.

That's all there was to it.

"TELL ME AGAIN WHY YOU have this beautiful house, but your Christmas tree comes out of a box," Jolene said that afternoon.

"It's no secret. First of all, have you noticed our ceiling?" He looked up to illustrate the point. "It's almost eleven feet in here."

"I see it."

"It's real hard to find a real, supersize tree. If we get a six or seven foot, it looks ridiculous. If we get one that's tall enough, it's harder than you can imagine to get the thing into the house and through the front door."

"So y'all went plastic."

Trent gripped one of the branches almost as if she'd made fun of his child. "This is real good quality, Jolene. We special ordered it from a fancy place."

"I can't wait to decorate it."

His expression eased. "Me, neither. And while you do that, I need to go do some shopping."

"I'll join you."

"Sorry, I need to do this on my own."

The way he was smiling at her made her realize his destination was no secret. He was going Christmas shopping. But just to make sure, she said, "Where are you going? When will you be back?"

Still looking full of secrets, he murmured, "I probably won't be back until dinnertime. I'll be gone at least a couple of hours."

"Oh. Well, I need to get some groceries."

"Feel free to take one of the trucks, or you can give me a list. I'll stop for you on the way home."

The roads were better and she did trust his truck a whole lot more than her sedan.

"I can go."

"You sure?"

"I'm going to make chicken fried steak for dinner."

The look of pleasure on his face was priceless. "Oh, honey. You do know the way to a man's heart."

Less than an hour later, he was gone and she decided not to put off the inevitable. After taking inventory in his massive kitchen and pantry, she made a list, found the pair of hundred dollar bills he'd left for her, got Amanda situated in the truck, and then made her first outing in one of the ranch trucks.

As Mrs. Riddell.

Just as she'd figured, the grocery store was busy. After saying hi to a few people, she made her way around the store, getting vegetables, baby formula, diapers and cubed steak.

Knowing how much Trent liked his desserts, she decided to make him a pecan pie. She'd just picked up a box of margarine for the pie crust when Addison Thomas appeared, a pretty brunette by his side.

"Hey, Jo," he said quietly.

Gripping the cart for support, she nodded. "Addison."

"This is Melissa."

"Pleasure to meet you," Jolene said, uncomfortable.

"How come you're all alone? I thought you were Trent Riddell's woman now."

There was no mistaking the hurt in his voice. But it was also obvious to Jolene that he'd never been all that taken with her...if he now was ambling through the grocery aisles with another girl. "I'm not his 'woman.' I'm his wife."

The brunette glanced at her left hand. "Congratulations," she said. But though she said the right word, she was doing that thing girls did...saying the right thing but looking as if they meant the exact opposite. "Do you have a ring yet?"

"Not yet. We were kind of in a hurry."

Addison had the gall to wink. "That's a shame."

Her tension over the situation couldn't have been more obvious.

With force of will, Jolene concentrated on Amanda. She was beginning to fuss, and she knew why. Amanda was used to her being happy. Not nervous and worried. When her little girl fussed in her carrier and her hands formed tiny fists, Jolene knew they were down to minutes before Amanda was going to have a full-fledged revolt.

"I need to go."

But instead of paying Amanda the slightest bit of attention, Addison looked her over with concern. It would have been sweet if it hadn't been misplaced. "Are you okay? Really?"

"I'm fine. Really."

"What's he going to do about the baby?"

She couldn't believe he was asking her such things.

In front of Melissa. In front of the whole store. "That's none of your business," she replied.

Next to her, Amanda gave up her fight as loudly and as pitifully as possible. Tears floated down her cheeks.

"I know, hon," Jo murmured, feeling as though she was about to cry herself.

Before Addison could make another comment, Jolene turned around.

She kept her head down and walked away, but if asked, she could have named every single person who had overheard their conversation.

WHEN SHE'D GOTTEN HOME, she'd received even more news. The doctor's office called and confirmed what she'd known all along, Trent Riddell was Amanda Rose Riddell's father.

"We'll be sending you the results in the mail, but with the holidays and all, I wanted to let you know now," the technician said.

"And I appreciate that."

"Do you want me to call Mr. Riddell, too?"

"No, I'll let him know."

Though the news should have made her feel like the happiest woman in the world, it somehow made her feel even sadder. She could only imagine the look that was going to appear in Trent's eyes when he was confronted with the proof.

He was going to feel relief…because there had been a part of him that had never believed her.

SHE WAS CHOPPING UP THE PECANS for the pie when Trent flew into the kitchen, a panicked expression on his face.

"What the hell happened at the store, Jolene?"

Her hands shook so much, she set down her knife. "What are you talking about?"

"I just got no less than three text messages saying that I'd better stop whatever I was doing and come see you. What happened at the store?"

"Nothing. I bought some groceries."

His eyes narrowed before he turned and shrugged out of his heavy barn jacket and hung it on a hook. "And?" he grumbled, his back to her.

"And...Amanda started carrying on something awful, so we scurried on out of there and I got her home." She felt her cheeks heat. Was she even home? "I mean, here."

But even that slip of her tongue didn't fool Trent. "This is home. I mean, it will be your home as soon as you get all moved in. Right?"

Before she could answer, he ran a hand through his hair. "Damn. Maybe I should've picked up the groceries for you. It's been so crazy, you should have taken it easy for a while."

"I've been going to the grocery store without you all my life, Trent. I didn't need you to go." Well, that's what she was trying to say. How it came out was more like a slur of words because her bottom lip had started to tremble.

And then the tears that she'd been holding back finally came.

After a pause, Trent circled the island. "Are you crying? Jo, *what happened?*"

She wiped a tear with her fist. "The doctor's office called. They got the results."

He searched her face, seemed to make a decision, and pulled her over to the kitchen table. "And?"

Oh, God. They were going to do this. "And you're absolutely Amanda's daddy."

He froze, so she started talking faster. "Do you believe me? The lady asked if I wanted her to call you so she could tell you herself, but I started thinking that would just be too weird."

He swallowed. "Yeah. I...I reckon you're right."

Unable to help herself, the tears started to fall again. "They're sending the official paperwork, too. She only called because mail delivery's going to be off, on account of Christmas and all."

"But it's official."

She nodded. And felt her heart just about sink to the floor. There was nothing in this situation that was right.

And so very much that was wrong.

Chapter Twenty-Six

They say the first time a man is bucked off the back of a bull is the hardest. That feeling of sailing through the air, flying for one second—though it seems like an eternity—is unforgettable.

There's the accompanying smell. The smell of fear from the bull, the scent of terror from yourself. The rest of a man's senses come alive, too. Dust, dirt and sweat cling to his face. The pounding from the rodeo clowns' boots seep into the ears. And then there's the knowledge that landing on the ground…and the sense that breaking a bone on the hard surface is the least of the worries.

Because what is most important—and most on a man's mind—is that he needs to get the hell out of the way as fast as possible. Before the bull finishes the job.

That is the adrenaline rush. That is that stuff that makes guys like him return again and again to the ring. It's not the buckle, or the girls, or the roar of the crowd. It's that incredible, amazing feeling.

The most intense feeling in the world.

But Trent realized that feeling was nothing compared to how he felt that very minute. It didn't even come close.

Now that he had the proof, he realized it didn't make a bit of difference. Deep inside, he'd known he was Amanda's father from the moment he'd seen those blue eyes. But instead of being a man and dealing with the truth, he'd been dancing around his responsibilities under the guise of being famous and rich, and therefore deserving of lab tests.

His behavior made him more embarrassed than he could ever remember being in his life.

Nervously, Jolene cleared her throat. "What are you thinking?"

That he wasn't good enough for her—or Amanda. "I…I don't have the words." Swallowing hard, he gazed at Jolene. She was still sitting on the edge of her chair.

As if she was expecting him to rehash everything about their night of Jack Daniel's, and her past and his self-centered piggishness.

Finally, Jolene broke the silence. "I think it would probably be best if I got Amanda and we left."

"Where would you go?"

"Where do you think?" she said, through a sad smile. "Home."

There was no way he was going to let her leave. "This is home now. This is your home. You married me," he announced, crossing the kitchen in a hurry to stand in front of her.

"Listen," he said. "We are going to be fine. You and Amanda are not going anywhere."

Tentatively, she placed a hand to his shoulder. "You're okay? So now that you have your proof, you're okay with being Amanda's father?"

There was only one right response, and he knew what it was, as sure as if his father had been standing beside him. Reaching for her hand, he said, "Right now I feel like the luckiest man on the earth."

"Oh, Trent. Oh, I'm so glad," she said, crying and blubbering and throwing her arms around him. "I thought you were going to get upset. Maybe even start yelling or something."

"I'd never yell at you."

"I know. You're so good to me." She lifted her head and met his gaze again, her green eyes beseeching.

"You should expect me to be good to you. You're my wife. You're the mother of my daughter. I couldn't be more happy."

If he didn't feel like the worst kind of loser imaginable.

But he was careful to keep none of that in his expression as he stared at her and smiled. "This is a wonderful day, Jo. A wonderful, amazing day."

That, of course, brought forth another round of tears, soaking his shirt right on through to his white undershirt. Her hands gripped his shirt in a death grip.

Gently, he loosened her fingers and splayed them flat along his chest. Shifting, she rested her cheek against the crook in his shoulder. Relaxing, finally.

He stepped a little closer. Gathered her closer in his arms. Whispered sweet things.

He held her tight because that was the right thing to do. And because he didn't want her sad. They had a lot to be happy about. He pressed his lips to her hair, to her cheek.

And then pulled away. "Why don't you go rest for a little bit? You can check on Amanda, I'll shower, and then you and I will make dinner together."

"You sure?"

"Positive."

She smiled at him, then walked away, leaving him alone.

He stood and walked to his room, stripped and turned the shower on as hot as he could stand it.

And then he stood under the spray and cried.

Chapter Twenty-Seven

At seven that evening, Jolene sat up with a start, then grabbed hold of her headboard when the room spun in circles around her. The room was dark.

Through her fog, she realized her drapes were closed.

Stumbling out of bed, she opened her bedroom door and hurried down the stairs, mentally chastising herself the whole way. She really shouldn't have slept so long.

"Trent?" she called out, turning the corner into the living room.

"We're here. Now settle down. You're going to scare her if you're not careful," Trent said from the couch. Patting the cushion beside him, he smiled slightly. "Why don't you take a seat, Jo? You're looking a little peaked."

She sat. "How long was I asleep?"

"A couple of hours."

She noticed he seemed just as calm and content to be sitting on the couch with Amanda as he had the first time she'd seen them together. "Has everything been okay?"

"Just fine. I fed her about an hour ago." Rubbing one finger down Amanda's chubby arm, he added, "The girl is fed and changed and enjoying ESPN with me."

"So I see."

"Do you mind if I hold her a little bit longer? She really is a cuddly thing."

Jolene shook her head, then realized he wasn't even looking at her. No, he was staring at Amanda Rose with enough love to fill the state of Texas.

"You love her," she murmured.

Slowly he looked her way. "I do."

The way he said those two words made Jolene's insides turn to mush. He was so calm now. So assured. Confident.

Now she was the only one without the right words.

"How are you feeling, honey?"

"Better."

He held out a hand. "Let's make a pact. After tomorrow, let's do our best to never discuss test results ever again. As far as I'm going to be concerned, you're my very sexy wife, and Amanda is my perfect daughter."

"After tomorrow?"

This time Trent was the one looking as if he was hiding a secret. "Well, I got on the phone and called my father."

Oh, dear Lord. "What did you tell him?"

"That I finally came to my senses."

"And?"

"And he was real excited," he said with a grin.

"How excited?"

"So excited that everyone's coming back tomorrow."

"Here?"

"Oh, yeah."

"Trent. What should I do?"

He regarded her seriously. "Well, while you've been sleeping, I've been doing some thinking."

"And?" She prepared herself for the worst. Did he

want her to go home for a while? Make her go stay in a guesthouse?

"I think we better put up that tree this evening."

"What?"

"Christmas is in two days, sweetheart. If everyone comes home and there's no tree for Ginny, I'm never going to hear the end of it."

"Trent, we can't be talking about decorating right now. Isn't your family mad? Don't you want to see them without me?"

"Jolene," he said, his voice turning all quiet and soft. "I don't care what my family thinks. I hope they'll welcome you with open arms. I hope they'll take one look at our little angel and decide I'm the luckiest guy on the face of the earth."

He leaned close and pressed his lips to her brow. "But even though I don't know for sure how they're feeling, I do know one thing."

"And what is that?"

"You're my wife, and if my family can't accept that, then to hell with them."

He meant that. He really did. Jolene felt humbled and dismayed, and oh, so pleased…all at the same time.

But instead of making a big deal about it, she got to her feet. "Well, then, let's get busy. We need to make dinner, put that tree together and start decorating."

As he got to his feet, he handed off Amanda. "I think that's a real fine idea. Let's get to work."

Chapter Twenty-Eight

His family wasn't necessarily thoughtful, considerate, polite or quiet. Sometimes they waited their turns when others were talking. Sometimes they even listened. But that was rare, and only on a really good day. And this, Trent decided, was not one of those days.

In what had to be a race against time, they arrived in a caravan of Ford trucks, his father and Ginny, followed by Serena and Jarred, then finally Susan, Hank and Cal. Each of them looking tanned and relaxed.

And, except for their father, completely at a loss for words about the latest development in Trent's life.

After a somewhat stilted round of hugs and introductions, Serena took the children, Jolene and Susan out to the barn to visit the horses.

Trent knew it had been at his father's request, but he was glad for the bit of privacy. What needed to be said didn't need an audience of ten.

While his father poured himself a glass of whiskey and Jarred and Cal looked him over and obviously were determining the best way to spout off their unwanted opinions, Trent decided to take control of the situation.

"Here's the thing," he said. "Jolene's my wife and

Amanda is my daughter. Y'all are just going to have to learn to accept that."

His father turned, met his gaze, then sipped a good half his drink. "I already did just as soon as I saw those eyes."

"Yes, sir."

"Are you sure that baby is yours?" Cal said.

"Positive. We, uh, got a DNA test. Even though I should have believed Jolene from the first, the test results proved it without a doubt."

Jarred's eyes narrowed. "You sound awfully calm."

"I love Jolene, and I love Amanda." He took a breath and blurted something that he'd only admitted privately to himself. "And even if Amanda hadn't been mine, I'd still stay married to Jo."

His brothers exchanged glances.

"It's not that we don't like her, Trent," Jarred said cautiously. "We do. It's just that, well, are you sure she didn't plan for this to happen? Are you sure she's not using you?"

"She is not."

Junior held up a hand. "I'm not saying it's her fault. You know how she was raised."

"She is not using me." His temper heating his every move, Trent stepped forward. It had been a long time since he'd hit one of his brothers, but that didn't mean he didn't know how.

His father's hand on his shoulder stopped him in his tracks. "Take a step back," he ordered. His voice was low and soft, but the unmistakable thread of steel was as apparent as ever. "Take a step back and take a deep breath."

Trent did as he was told, but he knew he couldn't take

enough backward steps and deep breaths to completely calm the anger he was feeling.

Jarred crossed his arms over his chest and glared. "You settled down yet?"

"Jarred, so help me—"

"Enough!" their father bit out. "Jarred, you and Cal need to apologize to your brother. Immediately. Jolene is his wife, and I was lacking in a lot of areas, but even I taught you two to respect a man's wife better than this."

A line formed between Cal's brows. "But, Dad. You can't think that—"

"Don't say a word except 'I'm sorry'," Dad said.

"I'm sorry, Trent," Cal said after a moment's pause. "I hope I didn't offend."

Jarred went one better and held out his hand. "I apologize," he said. "What I said was out of line."

Trent didn't think their words meant a damn thing. And he sure didn't need an apology that had been coerced out of them.

But he, too, had been brought up to mind his father. And so he went through the motions. All he had to do was excuse himself, then he could gather Amanda and Jolene and get them the hell out of there.

He held out his hand and shook his brothers' hands. Once that was done, he turned to his father. "I think I'll be going now."

"You'll do no such thing. Now sit down, and talk to me." He looked beyond Trent to where his brothers stood. "If you two can keep your fool mouths shut, you can stay."

All three of them sat.

"Now, talk to me, son," he said. "Tell me what happened after I left."

A lump formed in his throat. His dad's voice was as gentle as he'd ever heard it. And his posture was open and relaxed. With some surprise, Trent realized that his father really was making his best effort to understand.

Furthermore, he wanted to understand what had happened.

And that's when Trent realized that he wanted his brothers to understand, too. He needed this family. He needed it like he needed to breathe.

But just as important, he realized Jolene needed them, too. For almost all her life, she'd been standing at the outskirts, looking in. Taking scraps of affection when they were tossed out.

Never expecting more.

She deserved more than that. A whole heck of a lot more.

Choosing his words carefully, he said, "I'm going to tell you all that happened. Even though it's none of y'all's business. Not really. A little over a year ago, when I came back here, I was feeling full of myself and nostalgic. Jolene and I started talking, one thing led to another, and well…Amanda happened."

When Jarred scowled, Trent stilled him with a look. "Now, don't you start passing judgment, because I know for certain you've had more than one moment of weakness."

Looking away, his eldest brother nodded.

Then Junior leaned forward. "After that…moment… Jolene kept the truth from you?"

"No. She called me to tell me the truth…but I didn't take her calls." He looked at them, wishing he could find some reason to excuse himself, but he knew in his heart that there wasn't any. "I don't have a real good excuse, except that I was on the road, and there were a whole lot of other girls demanding my attention."

He shook his head in embarrassment. "But it wasn't the same for Jolene. See, she's always had a soft spot for me. Ever since I brought her home and gave her ice cream." He swallowed hard. "And let her hang out with us."

"She was just a tiny little thing," his dad murmured.

"Bruised," Cal said. "And too skinny."

"I used to sneak her Snickers bars," Jarred said. "She was always hungry."

Trent nodded, glad he didn't need to expound too much more.

"So she told you the truth, and you married her?" Junior asked.

"More or less. We spent time together, got that blasted DNA test, and then I realized I couldn't go another day before making things right.

"I married Jolene because she needed someone to believe in her," he stated, hoping the most important men in his family would finally understand. "I'm staying married to her because that feeling is growing stronger by the day. And every time I look at that baby, I know she's mine. Even without those test results, *I know it.*"

"I'd have to be blind not to see that that's my granddaughter," his father said gruffly. "And I ain't that."

Before he knew it, his dad had wrapped his arms around him. Immediately, Trent closed his eyes, let his father's familiar scent surround him. Give him strength. And, comfort. Not caring that his brothers were watching, Trent hugged his dad back and fought back tears. "So you're okay with this?"

Stepping back so they could see each other eye to eye, Cal Sr. nodded. "I'm better than okay. Trent, let me tell you a secret." He cocked an eyebrow. "You ready to listen?"

"Yes, sir."

"Your mother loved that little girl. *Loved her.*"

As Trent digested that, his father continued, his voice turning more gruff with each word.

"I can't tell you the nights she stayed up and stared out the window of our old living room, looking at the side of the Arnolds' house. Worrying about what was going on over there." He pursed his lips. "We called Social Services, even the police once when we saw the condition her mama was in."

"Anything happen?" he asked, though he was afraid he already knew the answer.

"Yeah. They moved." He paused, gathering his composure.

Trent darted a look at his brothers. They looked as stunned as he felt.

Finally his dad spoke again. "If it hadn't been illegal, your mother would've taken Jolene and given that girl a home." He sighed. "And now you have. I can honestly tell you that you've given your mother a mighty fine Christmas present, Trent. She would have loved that you married her."

Unable to stop himself, Trent blinked back a tear and hoped his brothers didn't notice. "She's a good woman, Dad. Real sweet and caring, too. And, she's a good mama to Amanda."

"To your daughter," his father corrected, hitting it home.

"Yes, sir. To my daughter. I didn't marry Jo out of pity. I…I want her to be my wife."

After clearing his throat, his dad slapped him on the back. "Of course you do, boy. You're lucky to have her." Standing a little straighter, he looked at them all. "Now, before we get all sappy, let us tell you what happened with old Pete."

"Did Paul uncover some news?"

"More than that," Jarred said with a smile. "It turned out that Pete had quite a bit of our equipment in a storage shed in town. He's been selling our stuff over the internet like he's freakin' eBay."

Trent couldn't believe it. "Wow."

Jarred grinned. "I think it made Paul's day to bring Pete in and charge him with a handful of felonies, if you want to know the truth. Nothing that big's ever happened in old Electra in decades."

"What did Pete say?"

"He confessed quite a bit before he lawyered up." Junior looked at him with a gaze full of respect. "We got him together, Trent. If you hadn't been checking things and asking questions, Pete probably would've continued for some time. We owe you."

"You don't owe me a thing. We're family," Trent said.

After some more discussion, their father stood. "Enough of this talk, let's go see those women. And I have a bone to pick with your wife, Trent. She hasn't let me hold that baby yet."

Cal winked as he left the room, following their father out of the house. Neither of them so much as wearing a coat on their way to the barn.

Beside him, Jarred paused. "Dad's right, you know…"

"About what?"

"Mom? Mom would've been tickled about this."

"I'm glad about that," he said simply. There was too much emotion in his throat to get much more out.

Chapter Twenty-Nine

Living with the Riddells was like nothing Jolene had ever known. The boys were loud and rough with each other and gentle with their women. Jarred constantly touched Serena, playing with the ends of her dark hair, or running a finger along her arm. And Cal, well, Cal seemed to thrive on battles of words with his wife. They'd talk and discuss and playfully argue over who was right. And the whole time they did it, their expressions would be bright with pleasure.

But what was most surprising to her was how Mr. Riddell acted with Amanda. The Mr. Riddell from her memories was larger than life and surly to the point of being rude. But the man who was sitting beside her on the couch was none of those things.

At the moment, he had his boots propped up on the coffee table across from them and her baby perched on his thighs. Amanda was looking up at him with a curious expression and wiggling her bare toes.

"She's about as perfect a baby I've ever seen, Jolene. She's sweet and adorable. Gorgeous," he said.

"I'm lucky," she agreed. "Amanda is easygoing and happy."

When Amanda circled his pinky with a tiny grip, Mr. Riddell grinned. "She's a strong one."

Ginny approached, crawling on the couch to her father's other side. "Was I that strong, Daddy?"

"You were. But you weren't never this sweet," he said with a wink. "You demanded attention from the moment you opened your eyes to the moment you closed them. Just about wore me out."

Jolene braced herself for the girl to get sad, the words were pretty harsh. But instead of crying, Ginny laughed uproariously. "It's a good thing we had my brothers, then," she said before scooting off. "They liked playing with me."

When she ran off with Cal and Susan's son, Hank, Mr Riddell stole a glance Jolene's way. "My daughter's a devil in disguise. She's gotten in more fights than the three boys put together."

"I wonder why?"

"She's scrappy. I need Trent to get her in the ring soon, to practice calf roping or barrel racing. Anything to keep her busy."

"Mr. Riddell, was Trent like that?"

"Nope. He was just good at everything physical. He could have played baseball or football…anything. But he was always calm." He gazed at Amanda some more. "Come to think of it, he was a lot like Miss Amanda here. Sweet and easygoing."

Thinking about Trent being a sweet baby made her heart melt. "Maybe that's where she gets her disposition from."

"Most likely. Now, when are you going to call me Cal like Serena does?"

Calling Mr. Riddell "Cal" would be like calling Santa

Claus "Kris." It just wasn't going to happen. "I can't. In my mind you're still Mr. Riddell."

"Well, that's no way to talk to your father-in-law." He thought some more. "Susan calls me 'Dad.' What do you think?"

Her father had been an awful man. But Cal Riddell Sr. was wonderful. "I'd like that."

He smiled broadly. "Me, too, honey."

"Me, too," Trent said from the doorway. "Because you really are a part of this family, you know."

Jolene turned to him in surprise. "I didn't see you there."

"I haven't been standing here long. Just long enough to hear the last of your conversation."

"Since I'm 'Dad' and all, you gonna let me hold our princess a little longer?" Cal Sr. asked, his gaze fixated back on Amanda, who was now almost smiling at him.

Jolene laughed. "You can hold her as long as you want."

"Well, hell. Look at this, our little girl is just about asleep."

"I'll go put her down." She moved to get Amanda.

"No, you will not. I can hold a sleeping baby just fine. Now, why don't you go on with your husband and get some fresh air?"

Trent scoffed. "It's twenty degrees out, Dad."

"Surely I don't have to make up activities for a new-lywed?"

"No, sir." With a grin, Trent held out a hand. "You want to go somewhere quiet so I can kiss you?"

Knowing he was teasing, she teased right back. "I thought you'd never ask." Turning to the man by her side, she said, "Dad, thank you." She didn't have to say for what. She and Cal Sr. knew. And, she realized, so did Trent. She was thanking him for everything.

He winked. "Anytime. Anytime at all."

To her surprise, Trent threaded his fingers through her hand and tugged her down the hall and out into the covered carport. And then he pressed her against the wall, his body heat warming her from head to toe.

Wrapping her hands around his shoulders, she said, "Are you really going to kiss me? Right here? Right now?"

Warm lips, so perfect and minty, answered that question. Without a single word spoken.

Chapter Thirty

Christmas Day was the prettiest one Jolene could remember. It dawned sunny and crisp, sending a glistening glow over all the trees, making them look as though the heavens above had decorated them for the holiday. Try as she might, Jolene couldn't find a single cloud in the sky.

But she had a feeling that even if it had been eighty degrees and raining, she would have thought this Christmas was the most wonderful. The most perfect. Because, at that very moment, Jolene knew for a fact that she was living in some kind of fairy-tale dreamworld.

"Jolene?" Trent called out from bed. "What in the world are you doing, standing over there by the window?"

She glanced his way, then let her gaze settle on Trent a little longer. Trent really did look pretty darn good, sitting bare-chested in the middle of the bed. "Nothing. I'm just looking outside."

"Well, come back to bed, honey. You're going to catch your death, dressed like that."

Looking down at her emerald-green negligee, her pajamas from the "Christmas elf" that Trent had said visited their bed last night, Jolene shook her head in mock aggravation. "I don't doubt I'm on the verge of getting frostbite. Somebody ought to tell that elf that it's December and not July. He should have brought me flannel."

Trent winced dramatically as she approached. "Jolene, it's becoming obvious that I'm gonna need to teach you a thing or two about the Christmas elf."

She let herself be tugged onto the mattress. "And what do I need to learn?"

"Number one, that elf doesn't buy flannel for anyone older than twelve."

"Only silk for ladies?"

"Of course."

"All right. I get that. But, you know, since it is December and all…maybe he should have splurged on more fabric."

Fingering the spaghetti strap on her shoulder, Trent reached down and pressed his lips there before he continued. "Number two, your Christmas Elf would never, ever, even think of covering up too much of you."

"And why is that?"

He shifted them so he was leaning over her. "Because you, Jolene Riddell, are absolutely beautiful." His eyes glinted. "And you look like my own personal Christmas present, all dressed up in green."

She felt like a Christmas present.

Or, well, maybe it was the other way around. She felt as if she'd been given a gift so big, it was almost too hard to handle.

Whenever she thought about the dinner the night before, Jolene knew she would tear up. Susan and Serena had treated her like a sister. And Cal Sr. in one hug, had given her the parent she'd always wished she had.

Even Jarred and Cal had seemed to come around. By dessert, they'd been teasing her as much as they teased Ginny.

"Jolene?" he ventured. "Jo, you okay? You went quiet all of a sudden."

"I'm sorry. I'm fine. My mind went drifting."

To her surprise, he shifted them both, settled with his arms around her and looked at her carefully. "Are you worried about something?"

"No. I was thinking about your family, and how glad I am that they accepted me and Amanda."

"Of course they would, honey. It just took time." He paused. "You're not worried about the two of us, are you?"

"Trent, after everything we've been through, I'm not worried at all."

The muscles in his arm tensed. She looked at him warily. "What's wrong?"

"I want to say something right, but I don't want to mess it up." Quietly, he said, "You gave me our daughter." He shook his head. "The way you sacrificed so much for Amanda, it takes my breath away."

For a second, she was sure her heart stopped. "I just loved her. That's all," she said finally.

And she'd loved Trent Riddell for most of her life, too. She'd loved him so much, she hadn't even cared that he didn't love her back.

She'd loved him enough for the both of them.

Long, lean fingers fiddled with her hair as he gazed at her. Slowly, he bent and brushed his lips to hers. "That reminds me. I've got something for you."

"Another present?" Already there had to be at least half a dozen presents under the tree with her name on them. "Trent, there was no need."

"Don't move," he murmured before walking to a leather satchel he'd left lying on the upholstered chair in the corner of the room. Two flaps opened, then he came back, a small black box in his hand.

As she watched him approach, she couldn't help but tease him about his red plaid pajama bottoms. "Someone needs to tell that elf about your no-flannel rule."

He winked as he crawled into bed. "I have a feeling you'll get me something better next year." Gathering her to sit in front of him, he held out the black suede box. "Hmm. I wonder what this could be?"

"There's no telling. You're spoiling me, Trent."

"That's impossible. You need someone fussing over you. Now hold out your hand and give me a smile."

She twisted so they were sitting next to each other. Their hips were almost touching, their legs were tangled, and the cozy flannel sheets were curled around them like a bird's nest.

She held out her hands.

He set the box in them.

Her hands closed, wanting to keep this moment forever.

He sighed. "Jolene, honey, I know that box is pretty, but the present is inside. Open it up."

Slowly she did as he asked. And gasped. Inside, was a wedding band, covered completely in diamonds. She was sure her mouth fell open as she stared. "Trent?"

"I've been racking my brain, trying to figure out the perfect wedding ring for you, Jolene. Doing the whole engagement ring thing seemed kind of silly, given the fact that, you know…we never really were engaged?"

Speechless, she could only nod.

"So then I got to thinking, well, a plain gold ring won't do, 'cause there's nothing plain about you. And then I started talking to the jeweler about these rings."

"The eternity bands?"

He looked pleased she remembered. "Uh-huh. See, the thing is, these eternity bands have symbolism to them. The diamonds going all around mean that the love is going to last forever."

Her breath hitched.

Blue eyes—the exact same shade as Amanda's—gazed at her. "And, well, that's when I knew this ring was going to be perfect, Jolene. Because I feel like you've been my girl forever."

"You—you feel that way?"

He nodded slowly. "I love you, Jolene. And the thing of it is, I think I always have. I loved you when we were small, and when all I knew was that I wanted you near. And I love you now."

"Because of Amanda?"

"Yes. But because of a lot of other things, too." He leaned closer. "Jolene, do you remember that day I went shopping?"

She shook her head. "Everything kind of seems mixed up now."

"I bought that ring before you told me about those test results," he said, his voice husky. "That baby girl is awesome—but I bought this eternity band for my sweetheart. I bought it for now. And for what we could become."

For what they could become. Her hand shook as she

took the band out of the box. Her fingers were shaking so badly Trent took the ring from her and carefully slipped it on her left ring finger.

She looked at him and smiled. "It's beautiful, Trent. I love it."

He grinned. "See, I told you so. Now, isn't that the best Christmas gift you ever got?"

That answer was easy. Almost too easy.

"It's not even close," she said. "The best Christmas gift I've ever gotten was you, Trent Riddell. You're my very own cowboy to love. My very own cowboy for Christmas."

Slowly, Trent lifted her hand, kissed the ring on her finger, and then pulled her close and kissed her hard.

And that's when Jolene Riddell realized that not another word needed to be said. Everything was as it should be. And it was all good.

* * * * *

HEART & HOME

Heartwarming romances where love can
happen right when you least expect it.

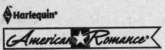

COMING NEXT MONTH
AVAILABLE DECEMBER 6, 2011

#1381 BIG CITY COWBOY
American Romance's Men of the West
Julie Benson

#1382 A RODEO MAN'S PROMISE
Rodeo Rebels
Marin Thomas

#1383 A BABY IN HIS STOCKING
The Buckhorn Ranch
Laura Marie Altom

#1384 HER COWBOY'S CHRISTMAS WISH
Mustang Valley
Cathy McDavid

REQUEST YOUR FREE BOOKS!
2 FREE NOVELS PLUS 2 FREE GIFTS!

 Harlequin®

 American ★ Romance®

LOVE, HOME & HAPPINESS

YES! Please send me 2 FREE Harlequin® American Romance® novels and my 2 FREE gifts (gifts are worth about $10). After receiving them, if I don't wish to receive any more books, I can return the shipping statement marked "cancel." If I don't cancel, I will receive 4 brand-new novels every month and be billed just $4.49 per book in the U.S. or $5.24 per book in Canada. That's a saving of at least 14% off the cover price! It's quite a bargain! Shipping and handling is just 50¢ per book in the U.S. and 75¢ per book in Canada.* I understand that accepting the 2 free books and gifts places me under no obligation to buy anything. I can always return a shipment and cancel at any time. Even if I never buy another book, the two free books and gifts are mine to keep forever.

154/354 HDN FEP2

Name _____
(PLEASE PRINT)

Address _____ Apt. #

City _____ State/Prov. _____ Zip/Postal Code

Signature (if under 18, a parent or guardian must sign)

Mail to the **Reader Service:**
IN U.S.A.: P.O. Box 1867, Buffalo, NY 14240-1867
IN CANADA: P.O. Box 609, Fort Erie, Ontario L2A 5X3

Not valid for current subscribers to Harlequin American Romance books.

Want to try two free books from another line?
Call 1-800-873-8635 or visit www.ReaderService.com.

* Terms and prices subject to change without notice. Prices do not include applicable taxes. Sales tax applicable in N.Y. Canadian residents will be charged applicable taxes. Offer not valid in Quebec. This offer is limited to one order per household. All orders subject to credit approval. Credit or debit balances in a customer's account(s) may be offset by any other outstanding balance owed by or to the customer. Please allow 4 to 6 weeks for delivery. Offer available while quantities last.

Your Privacy—The Reader Service is committed to protecting your privacy. Our Privacy Policy is available online at www.ReaderService.com or upon request from the Reader Service.

We make a portion of our mailing list available to reputable third parties that offer products we believe may interest you. If you prefer that we not exchange your name with third parties, or if you wish to clarify or modify your communication preferences, please visit us at www.ReaderService.com/consumerchoice or write to us at Reader Service Preference Service, P.O. Box 9062, Buffalo, NY 14269. Include your complete name and address.

HARIIB

*Lucy Flemming and Ross Mitchell shared a magical,
sexy Christmas weekend together six years ago.
This Christmas, history may repeat itself when they find
themselves stranded in a major snowstorm...
and alone at last.*

Read on for a sneak peek from
IT HAPPENED ONE CHRISTMAS
by Leslie Kelly.

Available December 2011, only from Harlequin® Blaze™.

EYEING THE GRAY, THICK SKY through the expansive wall of
windows, Lucy began to pack up her photography gear.
The Christmas party was winding down, only a dozen or so
people remaining on this floor, which had been transformed
from cubicles and meeting rooms to a holiday funland. She
smiled at those nearest to her, then, seeing the glances at her
silly elf hat, she reached up to tug it off her head.

Before she could do it, however, she heard a voice. A
deep, male voice—smooth and sexy, and so not Santa's.

"I appreciate you filling in on such short notice. I've
heard you do a terrific job."

Lucy didn't turn around, letting her brain process what
she was hearing. Her whole body had stiffened, the hairs on
the back of her neck standing up, her skin tightening into
tiny goose bumps. Because that voice sounded so familiar.
Impossibly familiar.

It can't be.

"It sounds like the kids had a great time."

Unable to stop herself, Lucy began to turn around,
wondering if her ears—and all her other senses—were
deceiving her. After all, six years was a long time, the mind

could play tricks. What were the odds that she'd bump into *him,* here? And today of all days. December 23.

Six years exactly. Was that really possible?

One look—and the accompanying frantic thudding of her heart—and she knew her ears and brain were working just fine. Because it was *him.*

"Oh, my God," he whispered, shocked, frozen, staring as thoroughly as she was. "Lucy?"

She nodded slowly, not taking her eyes off him, wondering why the years had made him even more attractive than ever. It didn't seem fair. Not when she'd spent the past six years thinking he must have started losing that thick, golden-brown hair, or added a spare tire to that trim, muscular form.

No.

The man was gorgeous. Truly, without-a-doubt, mouth-wateringly handsome, every bit as hot as he'd been the first time she'd laid eyes on him. She'd been twenty-two, he one year older.

They'd shared an amazing holiday season.

And had never seen one another again.

Until now.

Find out what happens in
IT HAPPENED ONE CHRISTMAS
by Leslie Kelly.
Available December 2011, only from Harlequin® Blaze™

Harlequin®

American ★ *Romance*®

LAURA MARIE ALTOM
brings you
another touching tale from

When family tragedy forces Wyatt Buckhorn to pair up
with his longtime secret crush, Natalie Poole, and care
for the Buckhorn clan's seven children, Wyatt worries
he's in over his head. Fearing his shameful secret will
be exposed, Wyatt tries to fight his growing attraction
to Natalie. As Natalie begins to open up to Wyatt,
he starts yearning for a family of his own—a family
with Natalie. But can Wyatt trust his heart enough
to reveal his secret?

A Baby in His Stocking

**Available December
wherever books are sold!**